Divyesh Mungra is a contemporary Indian author, young lyricist and former scientist. He chose to attend the long pending call of his heart, ending his stint in Medicinal chemistry research & development after achieving PhD and post-PhD degrees. As a scientist, he has worked with some giant organizations such as Lupin Pharma and Nanjing University. He published ten scientific research papers in journals of international repute.

He also has credits of writing Lyrics for television shows – Om Shanti Om (Star Bharat Channel), Shakti (Colors Channel), Billu Ustaad (movie), UMusicIndiaVEVO, Fiza-e-Ishq music album, 24 Carats Mithai Magic's advertisement jingle song and many more.

He immersed himself in honing his creative side and now revels in it. He believes he is blessed with an instinctive creativity which is best showcased through his story weaving.

This is his debut novel which he took around eighteen months to write.

Hailing from Gujarat, he currently lives in Mumbai. A few things that give him immense joy, apart from writing, are reading, music, movies, drama, road trips, tracking and playing badminton. He can often be found walking the streets of the world, in search of every form of beauty.

For more updates, join him on
Facebook (facebook.com/AuthorDivyeshMungra),
Twitter @DivyeshMungra and
Instagram @divyesh_mungra05

LET LOVE BE WEIRD

DIVYESH MUNGRA

Pengo
Publications India

Pengo Publications India
New Delhi 110078
Info.pengopublications@gmail.com

First published by Pengo Publications India

ISBN: 9788193225301

Typesett and layout by Ajay Verma
Printed and bound in India.

For

Pappa & Bapuji,

Who never stop

talking to me

Even after they entered the eternity

Acknowledgements

Thank you to all story hungry people for reading this book. A tight hug and two true tears for all those who are recommending this book to friends and their beloved.

Although it carries only my name, "Let Love be Weird" was produced through the efforts of many. Without them, this book could never breathe.

THANK YOU

to my mother,
For remembering to feed me when I couldn't remember to do it myself.
to Kunal,
For his support at every stage of my life.
to Namrata,
For her creative advices.
to Ruhaan
For always being close to me.

I would like to thank *Pengo Publications India* for taking a chance on this book and the hardworking team for their labor on it.

Big thanks to Prof. R. G. Patel for her guidance and encouragement.
Roopesh Kumar, you are a terrific human being. You guided me well so as to start my literary journey successfully. I owe it to you.

I am grateful to my friend Savvy Prabhat for helping me to grammatically edit my novel.
Rekha Mallya, thanks to keep reminding me that patience is a virtue and
"You can do it!"

I don't know how to thank my own memories of Department of Chemistry, Vallabh Vidyanagar, who helped me unlock so many doors and windows in this tale.

Thanks to my big gang of friends. Eventually, our bond is what keeps me going.

To those I couldn't mention, you know your hands were here, and
I thank you a hundred times more.

1.

Should I regret the table tennis ball sized fart? Or not? I don't know. Even though, the gas release was as silent as that examination hall we were sitting in, it disturbed me a little. I readjusted my round hips. Deadly smell of my fart mixed with the smell of *paan*, spreading from someone's mouth around me. I tried to exhale more and inhale less. When enough dilution of air had happened, I started filling out details on the answer sheet of my third semester M.Sc. exam.

Name: Shama Acharya
Roll no. : 24
Subject: Medicinal Chemistry
Department of Chemistry, Sardar Patel University

I heard someone whispering "butter-puff" behind. I ignored it. Why should I pay attention? I had more important things to do. Again doing my exam ritual, I was praying in whispers.

"God!" I closed my eyes and uttered repeatedly, "Please, help me to attempt at least half of the question paper."

Even though the green ink sketch of Sardar Patel printed on the corner of my answer sheet, kept staring at me. It never failed to scare me at every exam.

My preparation for that subject was minimal as set beside the huge syllabus.

"Butter puff, butter puff. I am sure today the girl's hostel had butter puff and tea at breakfast." I heard a teasing voice from behind.

This time it was little louder. Some nearby students had started laughing. One girl found it so funny that she had to hide her mouth by a handkerchief.

"Assholes," I shouted in my mind.

I looked back with wide-opened eyes to that stranger boy who was chewing the last bit of his *paan*. I kept staring at his reddish mouth. I wished he would be struck by my beautiful face. I was giving him some moments to turn his comment to some better inoffensive meaning. He had indirectly alleged me for that fart's smell of processed butter puff. And he was quite right.

"Don't you feel ashamed?" I said. "This is an examination hall."

"And it deserves clean air. But, why are you looking angry? Have you done it?" He squeezed his nostrils by his thumb and forefinger and said in a nasal voice, "If yes, say sorry like a frank girl."

"Huh! Frank girl." I repeated, mimicking his words, but, only in my mind.

I moved my sight on that class mate girl who was still laughing but it didn't affect her. The boy made a face as if he alone would have inhaled my whole fart.

"By the way," he said. "I am sure. It was you. I never speak a word until I am confident enough. Don't you think self-confidence is a must in examination hall?"

I didn't have any answer for his irrelevant and senseless question. Also, I never had any confidence whenever I appeared in examination hall.

The bell rang announcing eleven o'clock. The supervisor, dressed like a private bank employee except the tie, entered in and started distributing question papers hurriedly. Looking at him, I immediately felt as if my prayers had been heard. I checked my appearance and set a thankful smile on my lips. He spent a little extra time during giving me a copy. He blinked his left eye at me. I perfectly understood what he was telling by that.

It was, "Don't worry, baby! I am here now."

He was Ravin, a Ph.D. student in the same department. We were in touch from the beginning of the third semester. That 'touch' was a little more than just knowing each other.

Just before a week, when practical exam was over, I thanked him for helping me extremely well in a difficult experiment, which was given for the final exam.

"Medicinal is my main problem." I had asked for his favor in my special way. "If you can solve it anyhow, we can think to have some leisure time together."

He assured me he would try to be present as a supervisor in the medicinal paper to let me glimpse my chits freely from the gaze of nearby students. He truly tried and managed to be there.

I just wanted to pass the exams and get a degree. I never dreamed to be a topper. I believed that my memory capacity was not bigger than a table tennis ball. Even if I push my limits, it would remain a tennis ball and never be a football.

So, I always focused to use the things which I already had. Naturally. Effortlessly. God had gifted me with beauty. I am not fond of boasting over my beauty. But I can say it was a kind of weapon at the face of others, which was impossible to hide. And yes, it never failed whenever I used it.

I had carefully chosen my words as there was one more semester to pass. I knew what meaning of my words "leisure time together" Ravin understood.

So, before he could plan anything, I booked movie tickets for the afternoon show. I chose two seats in the middle and not towards any corner. When I showed him the tickets, he tried hard to hide his first reaction. He looked defeated as if I would have failed all of his plans very badly. But soon he recovered. He gave me three hundred rupees.

"You are still an unemployed student, Shama," he said. "I have a research-fellowship of sixteen thousand per month."

Before I could try to convince him, he opened my fingers, put money and closed my fist. He touched my hand with such an ease as if he had earned an official right on me by helping in exams. I agreed on taking money without any opposition. I didn't want him to begin touching me so easily except for the hands.

During the movie, I was so restless that I couldn't keep following the story of such a good movie "*Veer-Zaara*." I saw the full movie being restless. For the first time, someone i.e. the boy chewing the *paan* had ignored my beauty. Not only ignored, that unknown boy teased me in too bad a way. In some sense, that boy had damaged my long time confidence over my beauty.

Ravin didn't seem to try to come nearer. Perhaps he was too unhappy with my choice of seats. It is quite possible, he thought of getting "everything or nothing at all". I kept silent with my hands folded.

Finally, I showed a little hope to him in the last moment.

"Well," I said. "We should choose a peaceful place where we can talk instead of watching a movie. Isn't it?"

He agreed.

When we were coming back on his *Pulsar*, even though he was not using disc brakes at all, I had slightly fallen towards him two times. It was necessary to keep him hooked about me.

To reach the goal of being a postgraduate with zero efforts, my beauty was working for me as a ladder. Lazy me, I didn't wish to interfere!

2.

I had developed a kind of artificial shyness inside of me. According to my mother, it was an important part for my looks and was meant to be a life strategy. I often heard from her that the shyness of a girl is an ornament that will never go out of fashion.

She told me with wet eyes, after the second heart attack of my father.

"You have to settle before the third one. Otherwise I will have my first one. Shama? Do you understand our situation?"

She kept increasing her frequency of the heart attack as a reminder to me while I passed from semester to semester. She never had a problem with my poor grades.

I had just entered my final semester.

I saw my mark sheet of third semester and forgot my long practiced shyness for a while. I almost jumped as high as I could. I had passed it without any need of an exemption. There was a little star showing "exempted" in both of my earlier semester results. But now in third semester, there was no little star. I passed it with dignity, at least in comparison with my earlier performances.

My happy mood and continuous chitchat with my friends were disturbed when I saw that shameless *paan* chewing boy coming towards our group. We were reviewing each other's mark sheet in the parking area of the department. He parked his big twenty-four number old atlas bicycle near me and gave me his mark sheet.

"Show me yours," he said as if it was an ordinary exchange.

I saw he had scored more than double of my marks in all subjects. I really didn't want a word with him. But, my mark sheet made me to forget all those things for a while. So, like a shy and polite girl, I congratulated him, without shaking any hands.

"Oh, you have got really good marks," I said.

My intention was just to shorten our conversation and let him leave our group as soon as possible. I tried it hard to find a way not to show him my mark sheet. But before I could say anything, a girl who was already studying my mark sheet, gave it to him.

"What did you say? Good marks?" he laughed while reviewing my mark sheet. "Don't you know I have topped this semester. Your HOD, what is his name? Whatever it is, he has invited me to meet him."

He instantly grabbed full attention of our whole group.

"I topped in spite of that bad butter puffed atmosphere," he went on insulting me.

I knew he was saying this sentence to me particularly. I wished to slap him on the spot. But slap would have confirmed to the others about my gross act of farting. So I kept quiet and gestured like other girls who weren't able to understand what he said.

"Meaningless mark sheet. What was that which made you look so happy?" he said, giving my mark sheet back. And then, he went away after bursting the balloon of my happiness.

* * *

He was from the other M.Sc. (Chemistry) department which was under private institutions. But, it was affiliated to our Sardar Patel University.

I started spotted him in my department since last week. I wanted to know why he was coming to our department every day. Perhaps he had been trying to meet Prof. Shardul, Head of department.

My department was the oldest and a highly reputed one among all the institutions which were running the same postgraduate course. It happened for the first time in history that someone from any private institute topped in final university exams. So, that boy generated a lot of curiosity in my department.

I heard some strange gossips about him in the brief gatherings in our practical lab. Initially, I thought it was just a rumor. But, I had to believe it when my room partner girl gave me an overused audio cassette. There was a roughly handwritten warning on it.

"LISTEN ONLY, WHEN YOU ARE LONELY (1)"

In this warning statement, the feel of warning was less and the invitation to listen was more. Whoever got that cassette was quickly found in search of a lonely place and a walkman with ear phones. Being lonely was a difficult thing in the hostel. Walkman was also a rare and costly thing. But, we all had managed to get it by any means.

I started hearing that cassette in a Sunday afternoon in my hostel room. I immediately recognized the voice of that shameless *paan* chewer. The words were different but the tone was exactly the same as that of "butter puff, butter puff" whispering which I hadn't forgotten. Gradually, the whispering became a clear cut voice. The content of that story being told was so adult and sensual that my ears were getting red due to real shame. After the middle part, I was forced to imagine being with someone handsome and doing whatever the characters of that audio story were doing. I don't know why but that "someone handsome" was Ravin.

* * *

Prof. Dr. Shardul was our HOD. Perhaps he had celebrated his fifty-fifth birthday, alone in his duplex provided by the university. He was unmarried; reasons unknown. The couples, who believed in showing off the act of love making, had always disturbed him. Perhaps that was the reason why he never bought television. The department kept arranging a movie screening once every year in our igloo shaped auditorium but he never attended. Whenever he saw boys and girls into conversation, he made a face as if that conversation would turn them into future happy couples within no time.

When our second semester had just been started, he was promoted to the post of the HOD; not at all by performance, but totally by seniority. I mean this is an Indian government institution. On the very first day after he took charge, the first rule he made was that, boys and girls have to sit away from each other from the next day. Everyone read those bold large sized letters in the notice board. It disappointed some students also. But no one had a sentence to argue with him.

"Why do you want to sit near your antagonistic gender?" What if he asked back?

And about his English, even his twenty five years of teaching experience couldn't improve his choice of words.

For example, if he would have written that notice by his own hand, he would write, "Boys and girls will be cut by a sharp space."

But I had no problem with it. My seat was fixed on the first bench with my roommate who was a girl.

It was an ordinary day. I was entering my class room at 11 a.m. I couldn't believe what I saw. That same *paan* chewer was sitting on my roommate's place next to my seat. My roommate was absent on that day.

"May I ask you what are you doing here? I mean in our department," I said, keeping my voice low and gentle.

"Yes, I allow you to ask. Ask anything," he said, smiling over my irritation.

"So, please tell me what are you doing here?" I said, frustrated but controlling my temper.

"M.Sc. Chemistry, forth semester," he said. "Your HOD, what is his name? Whatever! He has requested me. Sorry, he begged me to join this department. May be he doesn't want someone from any private institute to top again in this final semester. So, I am here to save the reputation of this department."

Even though his point was convincing, I couldn't imagine that Shardul Sir could request for anything to that shameless creature.

I concluded that this is why he was coming every day- for official procedure of his transfer from private institute to our reputed central government institute.

In a blink of eyes, I predicted that this whole semester would be a difficult time. Five months of a single semester seemed as a life time problem.

It was 11:03 am i.e. the regular arrival time of Shardul Sir. I didn't wish to witness any scene which could drag me unnecessarily into trouble.

"See, we have official rule that boys and girls sit separately," I said. "Can't you see how others are sitting?"

"Why are you worrying so much? I am not sitting on your place," he answered.

In spite of grabbing too many eyeballs, he went on.

"It should be enough for you. By the way, I have a responsibility to top again. It is necessary for me to sit on the first bench."

We heard the prayer being sung from the loudspeaker. "*Hamko man ki shakti dena, Man vijay kare...*" We all stood up and closed our eyes.

Shardul Sir's gesture came to my mind. Freshly combed hair, oiled by a, one is to one mixture of *parachute* oil and water. Black framed spectacles with soda bottle glasses.

He just entered and stood up between the doors to speak his prayers. He couldn't close his eyes unless the first stanza of the song finished. He had fixed his sight on our first bench. I felt the weight of his anger over my closed eyes. My thoughts were disturbed to such an extent that meaningless thoughts came to my mind.

"Oh God! Why did you force me to fart that day?" I said to myself.

"*Bharat mata ki . . .*" that shameless dog of a guy beside shouted, as and when prayer completed.

"*Jay . . .*" No one replied except him.

He roared like the hooligans shout after the national anthem is sung in cinema halls. My heart skipped a beat and suddenly the pace doubled. Everyone predicted that Sir would start scolding him. But the arrow had been fired from an opposite direction than our expectation.

"Siddharth, this is not a cinema hall and you are not watching a movie," said Shardul Sir calmly.

Sir already knew and remembered his name. I didn't like it.

"But, it is a movie song from the movie *Guddi* released in 1971. *Sangeet hai Vasant Desai ka aur bol hai, Gulzar ke,*" said Siddharth.

Everyone recognized his old radio anchor type tone. Only half of us succeeded to hide the laughter.

"I don't see films," said Sir.

"But, just due to your ignorance, this filmy song can't be a prayer."

We were surprised by the calm Shardul Sir had kept. It seemed as if he had really begged him for joining our department. May be Sir had decided to kill him by rule.

"We have a rule that antagonistic gender keeps a space between them in the classroom," Shardul Sir said, hoping the end of arguments.

No one laughed as we all had developed an understanding to catch the meaning of Shardul Sir's language. Siddharth was new. Even though he didn't laugh, he had another argument.

"Does this department think that just by sitting closer, girls become pregnant?" he said. "No! My dear, ignorant people.

No. There is a different procedure for that."

He started glowing by his knowledge. He looked too happy with his argument. His face showed clear cut lines of pride as if he had just now cleared a great ancient misunderstanding of our department about how to make girls pregnant.

"Now we both will not be visible to each other in this class room for two future weeks," said Sir in a decisive tone.

"Umm . . . sorry Sir, my English is very poor," he said. "I didn't get you. You mean you will not come here. Or I shouldn't come?"

Each of us felt that now was the time of the final moment.

"You, you. You came to me to join this department and requested for a whole week. I hadn't sent you any invitation card. Now get lost," Sir said. I liked that finally Sir had shown his original self.

Siddharth was walking out without his *Puma* handbag.

Just by indicating a finger, Shardul Sir asked him to take his bag with him.

"Let me keep it here, Sir. For next lecture," said Siddharth while walking out without it. He acquired the body language of a century hitter batsman, going to pavilion.

He proved my word to the point-"Shameless."

"Because of you all," Shardul Sir said after he left. "I am deleting him for only two weeks. What to do? I don't have a trust on any of you to top in this final semester. If I would have, I would have erased that boy forever from our department.

3.

I suddenly received shocking information about Siddharth. Yes, it was shocking at least for me. It was that, his name was "Siddharth" and my name "Shama." Alphabetical order "Sh", then "Si". According to that, it was quite possible that he could be my lab partner during practical sessions. His name had power to replace my earlier lab partner Suhani. New possible order would be ". . . Sh, Si, Su . . ." It became reality in afternoon practical session. Our attendance sheet was rearranged.

There was no Shardul Sir's antagonistic gender rule for lab. Students were arranged as per alphabetical order. That's may be because Shardul Sir had never visited the lab. He kept himself to his cabin, his Ph.D. research lab, class room and canteen only. No one had ever seen him at M.Sc. final's lab, igloo auditorium or play ground for sports day events. Also teaching in practical sessions was a thing outside his capability. There was a believable rumor that he had got that lecturer job before twenty-five years just because of him belonging to the lower caste quota.

When we all were provided our practical work space in the lab, I found Siddharth stood at Suhani's place. I decided to have a decent, little conversation because I had to pass that last semester bearing him anyways.

The relationship of lab partners is like that of two halves of a pair of earphones. They always had to stay together but could change positions as for the magnet inside each of them.

"Hey Sid," I said. I used a popular nickname for his name, in hopes of starting with some closeness. "We will be working as lab partners for this whole semester. So, I thought of chatting."

He didn't react. I thought he wanted a little more buttering up. So, I went on. "It's great to have you, the topper."

"Shama," he said. "Just because we are lab partners, you want to talk to me? I was thinking you would be dying to have a word with me. In my department, I mean earlier one, girls were like that only."

"Yes yes," I said with extra fake shyness. "I can imagine that. I think I am a little shyer girl than the other girls."

"I don't think so," he said. "I saw you falling shamelessly from back seat towards Ravin. I think you people were coming back after watching *Veer-Zaara*."

He shocked me by revealing that he knew too much in detail about me. I immediately checked if the nearby classmates were listening to us or not. Yes, some were. I felt really embarrassed now. I realized that we were at the dead end of a conversation. But he proved me wrong by going on.

"Anyway, we should know each other little well as we are lab partners, right? Then listen. I like girls like you, Shama, who can play both, being shy and shameless depending upon the need. But in spite of having a vast experience of those romance games, I can't understand what you saw in that boy? I mean he is a Ph.D. student under the guidance of Shardul Sir. That's it. Isn't this enough of information to judge him? He drives him every day from his home to department on bike. What is he? Researching driver or driving researcher? Whatever he is, but, he is not less than a fool for sure. And look, he's here seemingly just arrived from some private bank."

He pointed a finger towards Ravin. He was coming towards me.

Ravin, again dressed like a private bank employee except the tie, started talking to me and ignoring everyone else. He congratulated me by shaking hands.

In our department, Ph.D. students were like half-professors. They had some local administrative powers to behave as professor. Ravin had a habit of using it frequently.

"So, baby is happy now. I saw your result on the internet. No little star on mark sheet," said Ravin.

I rolled my eyes and gave an expression giving away my shyness. Then Ravin went away like the professors who always talk to the point. No more. No less. By meeting me in front of everyone, he was indirectly indicating to anyone who might have an interest in me, that I was occupied. As if someone reserves his seat by putting a handkerchief from the window of a bus.

"Hmm ok," said Siddharth. "Now, I got it. He was our supervisor in Med. Chem. paper. Right?"

"What right do you have to judge anybody?" I said. "I have also heard your cassette of that dirty audio story. For two minutes." I regretted after saying it.

It was enough for him to catch my mistake.

"But, my dear Shama, in first two minutes there is nothing dirty. I doubt you have listened to it more than that? Or maybe more than half? Or . . . full? Or twice? Or . . . on repeat mode?"

"Shardul Sir did the perfect thing for you," I said. "You deserve that only. And what were you telling? Sir begged you to join here. You liar!"

For that question, he didn't answer me, confessing that he himself had begged Shardul Sir for letting him join our department. With that sentence, I had lost hopes of being in better terms with Siddharth.

"So, who is perfect?" he said. "Shy girl? Or dirty audio story teller, or the unmarried high quality English professor? Or that boy who tells you "baby"? What is his name?"

That clever and short conclusion cleared the whole point of discussion between us. Everyone's character certificate was in need of that little star of exemption.

When our eyes met, I laughed more than a shy girl should. It was a natural laugh. Purposeless! Not done for getting in good terms with anyone. Several lab mates looked our way. They may have been surprised to see both of us talking with such delightful faces. Especially, since that morning of our heated argument in the classroom. Siddharth was looking at me with teasing eyes like that of a small boy's.

* * *

In the lab, Ravin came like a wind and went. But something flicked in my mind. I realized it later. Like someone opens a "new tab" in Google chrome, he had clicked that key inside me. His style of glancing over me reminded me of the time, when I was forced to remember him while I was halfway through the story being told in that cassette in Siddharth's voice.

I again found some alone time and a walkman with ear phones in my hostel room. At that stage, I can assure that my fantasy took a perfect shape of a real story and characters. This time one little thing was changed. Ravin became a character from the beginning of that audio story. I fantasized that I would have removed his entire private bank employee like clothes. And I expected similar things from him to do with me.

One day, he saw me alone near the water cooler, in the department. Before I could paint any physical colors on my fantasy, he came to me.

"Baby," he said, without exactly looking at me. "I have found a peaceful place where we can talk. It would be better instead of wasting time in the cinema hall."

There was no reason to deny. I myself had insisted him to find such a place after watching *Veer-Zaara* together. But why should I refuse him? I already wanted him while doing *things* with myself during listening to that dirty audio story.

"Please take me to that place immediately," I wanted to tell him.

But my so-called shyness forced me to say something different. "Oh, you have found a place. Good. I will let you know when I can come."

After a little more casual chit chat, he left with the feeling of a merchant failing in the collection of money.

4.

Since the beginning of my graduation, I was residing in the university girl's hostel. I reached that small town called "Vidyanagar" near Vadodara for my education, which was 250 kilometers away from my hometown.

That time cell phones were the status symbol and luxury. And my family did not belong to that rich class. In our hostel, we were not allowed to keep cell phones. We had a common landline phone whose outgoing facility was disabled when one day our rector saw the sudden bounce in the bill. He found out that hundreds of outgoing calls had been tried to Amitabh Bachchan's television show "*Kaun Banega Crorepati*." Numbers on the dial pad were almost blurred. I, in spite of having a small memory and zero general knowledge, regretted not having grabbed a free chance to call that show. We were provided fixed time and interval to attend a call from our parents.

On my turn on Saturday night, my mother called me. Her voice seemed tired that day. I knew the reason perfectly; because I was in my last semester and yet not settled, according to her definition. She told me all the stuff which she kept telling me in every phone call from last four and a half year, every Saturday.

"Shama, we have sent you there for making a life. Not just to earn a random degree. And I am sure you can. You will. Take care of your skin and figure. But, don't forget to look shy. It never fails. You know, I spotted some of your old schoolmates still circling about our street to catch glimpse of you only, my daughter."

When I answered her, she went speechless.

"Mamma," I said. "Tomorrow I am going to meet a suitable boy in person."

And then, after hearing the whole thing excluding my fantasy part, she told me in a low worried tone. I am sure she was happily worried.

"Call me from any STD booth after meeting him."

* * *

It was an evening of Sunday, six o'clock. Though there was no need; I had covered my face with a white and saffron scarf and eyes with black goggles. I don't know what Ravin felt about my look, but he only recognized me when I sat on his bike with a little jump. In just six minutes, we were out of our small town. The town was so small that to use the word "town" seems unfit. We were heading towards the place Ravin had discovered. We both were silent. We had such an 'intention' which makes one silent specially when doing it for the first time.

I couldn't welcome the change he did in himself.

Firstly, he wore a sky blue t-shirt. Secondly, he had used body spray. Both changes were shoving my version of fantasy which had now taken an exact shape from Siddharth's audio story.

But the jolt was not enough for me to order Ravin to go back or postpone.

On the way, I saw the same cinema where we had seen *Veer-Zaara* earlier.

"Ravin," I said. "Stop here. We have to buy a movie ticket."

He stopped on the side.

"The place I found is really nice for talking peacefully," he said, looking at me in the right mirror of his bike. "You will like it, Shama. And we will reach there in ten minutes. But it's ok. Your wish! You told me to find a place. Isn't it? Also, I don't think any good movies are there. See those posters."

I found him much defeated but not unhappy. I was really surprised by his patience. But, he had misunderstood me.

"I took permission from hostel for allowing me to reach back late night," I said. "Our hostel has a rule that if any girl comes after 11.30 in night, she have to prove where she was. It's not too strict but sometimes our rector asks."

We bought a ticket as a proof. He didn't tell me but he looked content and brightened after knowing we had enough time. And most importantly, he liked how perfectly I was managing that amount of time in which our intentions could be fulfilled well.

Finally, we left the highway and he drove on a narrow one way. He parked his bike on the shore of the canal. Everything was as silent as the smoothly running water in the canal. The sky was clouded with some rays of sunlight. I removed my scarf from the face and stretched my body.

"Do you keep a water bottle whenever you go out?" he asked.

"Yes, but I forgot today," I said.

"Let's have some water from the canal. It's drinkable," he said.

I reached the bank of the canal and sat down to drink the flowing water. Ravin followed me. Our reflections from water were also mimicking us. Flowing water couldn't wash out our flowing intentions.

He started walking towards the trees on the other side. I followed him. We were continuously checking around to assure that we are alone. Scenes from Sid's erotic audio story were beginning to get shapes in my mind. We stood under a big tree.

He was in no hurry, but I had stopped myself for too long.

"Do you have everything we may need?" I asked.

My question confirmed the green signal for him. He pressed his pants pocket and showed a square shaped packet from inside.

"Yes baby," he said.

He started removing my *salwar* from below side. He was so close that my nostrils filled with the strong smell of his body spray. Both of those things- way of removing my *salwar* and fragrance of that body spray didn't fit into my imagination of the erotic story on the audio.

"No, Ravi. Not like that," I said and shrank a little.

He left my *salwar*. He took my face in his hands gently and we found ourselves on the edge of our first kiss.

"No, *yaar*. What are you doing?" I said.

My disappointment couldn't find a place to hide. According to my fantasy, initially, he should sit behind me, press me by both of his hands, start kissing from the edges of my ear and play a bit with my earrings, keeping himself behind me.

I could instruct him about how I would like to move ahead. But, I didn't because even if I would have told him, there was no escape from that smell of body spray. An artificial smell. I liked his original body odor on the bike whenever we had a ride together.

Even the erotic audio story had a moment for advocating original fragrance of the body. How could Ravin understand my expectations? He never heard that story. Finally I had to tell him some undesirable words.

"I told you to find a peaceful place for talking. Isn't it? Let's sit there," I said, pointing towards a small bridge over the canal.

I had already started walking away. I hadn't seen, but I am sure he might be struggling to adjust his woken up *thing* inside his underwear. We sat on the bridge hanging our bare feet. We immersed our legs in cold moving water passing through the canal. I believe the coldness of the water had helped me to forget or postpone my intention. It was like overflowing desire was descending to heels and getting washed out smoothly.

"I've never been so confused," he said. He sat beside me, but not close enough. He took out a square packet labeled "*Kohinoor*", cut all three pieces and threw all of them in water.

"Ravin," I said.

He didn't wait for my words and said, "It's about making life, not earning any qualification."

I was surprised at his words which were from my mother's dictionary. It reminded me that I would be calling her tomorrow. And what would I say?

"Nothing happened, Mamma. Because… because … I don't know how to say it."

I immediately planned to manage things again. I took Ravin's hand gently in my own.

"Ravi," I said. "You are more than any degree and life."

I took his face between my palms, closed my eyes, stopped breathing for a second, kissed mildly on his lips, tried to ignore the strong smell of his body spray, and established something, against which Ravin's confusion couldn't stand. I confirm that it was a mild kiss. Or a compromised one. I didn't feel any passion during the small contact time of our lips. There was an air bubble between us. There wasn't created vacuum between four lips.

In short, we can't say nothing had happened. Also, we can't say everything had happened.

While coming back, we were just as silent as we were when going. But the reason was different. I reached my hostel too early. The rector had no reason to ask anything. I threw that movie ticket in the dustbin. I brushed my teeth, took a bath, and washed my lips a little more than usual.

5.

Next morning, while going to the department, I called my mother from a yellow STD booth. She attended the call just after first ring and said, "What happened?"

"Mamma," I said. "We had spent around two hours together."

"No matter how long you were together. But with which kind of feeling you left after the meeting is important. Isn't it?"

"Yes yes, Mamma," I chose my words while saying. "We are progressing."

I had never lied to that helpless woman, but sometimes I had to compose a sentence which could have multiple dimensions. Whenever I did that, she always found out her own correct dimension in a fraction of a second.

"If you have any doubt about the success, keep an option. Your father wants to see you both as soon as possible," she said after a little pause.

I thought of my father's blessing to me after his second heart attack.

"Make a life my daughter. Make a life," said dad with wet eyes, while I was leaving home for my post graduation.

After reaching Vidyanagar, when I telephoned my mother, she explained the hidden meaning of my father's blessing which she thought was right.

"It's the only way a father can say this thing to his daughter. Do you get me? Make a life means find a suitable boy," said Mamma.

Though I agreed to keep an option, I couldn't see any better option for making a life.

* * *

I was about to enter the main gate of the department. I saw a black Royal Enfield Bullet pass by me and almost touch my *dupatta*. Siddharth parked it with a sudden roar. Some days ago, I spotted him parking a big, overused, dilapidated 24 numbered Atlas bicycle.

I had two important reasons for being nice to Sid. Firstly, he knew that I was progressing with Ravin. He had already seen me on the back seat of Ravin's *Pulsar*. Sid could spread this information which can possibly harm my "shy girl" image and thereby limit my options to get settled. Secondly, he was my lab partner, means I had to pass twenty hours a week with him during practical sessions.

In the lab, I took a deep breath of the mild chemical smell. I started talking to Sid in the sweetest voice I could manage.

"Hey Sid, your new bike really suits you," I said.

"Why don't you say what you are really thinking?" He looked at me with surprise and said, "I thought you would ask, hey Sid, which one is yours? Bicycle or bullet? Or both?"

I confirm that he was in his old mood with that strange attitude. So, I decided to play safely.

"Well, that question was in queue," I said.

"My bike is not new. I have it since last three years. For a week, I borrowed that bicycle from our hostel's gatekeeper just to come in the sight of Shardul Sir with a little poor look. Immediately after he showed me with bicycle, I met him in his office with my mark sheet. I was just fooling him. You see, it worked."

I nodded. And then he came so close to me that I could hear his breathing. Even my earring moved a little by his exhale.

"Actually it didn't work," he said.

"Then?"

"Sir had no problem with the fact that someone from a private institute topped. In fact, he genuinely congratulated me. Do you want to know what he said? He said, Siddharth, you obtained the top floor. Good, good. I am happy that personal institutes are doing better."

"Hahaha… Did you understand his words? Top floor and personal institutes?" I said. Now, I had started adding smiles with my blushes.

"Yes, I had to suppress my laughter," Sid said. "But he hadn't begged me for joining here. I also never begged to him. No one will ever know the real thing between us. You may try to investigate. If you succeed, you will come to know that the head of this department had nothing in his head except empty space."

"But in the first place, why were you so interested to join here?" I asked.

"That's because of two reasons. One is you, shy girl. And another, you will know someday."

"Sid, we are lab partners for the whole semester. We are now becoming good friends. Don't you think we should be frank with each other?" I said without meeting his eyes.

I just wanted to find out a better quality secret about him, which would help me to control him from spreading my secret about Ravin.

"Yes sure. I am already frank with you. Do you forget our first conversation? You farted and all that. If I am not frank, I couldn't talk about farting with you. Isn't it? But very soon, you will see my real version of frankness," he said with teasing eyes.

I thought, "Oh god! What does he have in his mind now?" I couldn't find a chance to tell him what I really wanted to, even though it was urgent.

Before I could plan any more about it, our lady Professor Dr. Padmini came out of her small cabin attached to our lab. She spread her celebrity smile, especially to Siddharth and announced in an authoritative but sweet voice.

"I already instructed you all to prepare a proposal for the independent research project for this final semester, right? So today, you all will pitch it to me. Let's meet and have a fruitful discussion on it in our auditorium."

We were informed that out of two lab partner's proposals, Padmini Madam would choose one. On that decided project, both lab partners must work together. Padmini Madam had introduced that extra thing just after she was given charge of our practical sessions. No one liked it but no one ever opposed because she had useful contacts with some big multinational pharmaceutical companies, which were in our dreams for the job. She was manager in research & development department of *Lupin* Pharma before joining our department as a professor.

Whole department knew that she could easily drag companies to conduct campus interviews in our department. Her career was as bright as her celebrity smile. She had cleared NET (National Eligibility test) exam consecutively six times. There was a rumor that she had written to UGC (University Grant Commission) that they should improve the toughness of question paper. How can one girl pass it every single time?

Siddharth became her favorite student in just two weeks.

I really failed to understand why Sid never paid as much attention to theory classes as he did for practicals. He was visiting Padmini Madam in her cabin at least three times in a single practical session of four hours. Honestly, I never saw Sid wasting time during practical periods like me and most of us. Either he would be busy in experiments or he would be in Madam's cabin.

Madam had even appreciated him once in front of everyone.

"Siddharth have found out why we always get lesser yield while preparation of *Coumarin* perfume. Everyone should correct the method in personal record books as per Siddharth's method," said Madam.

After that Sid had permission to visit Madam without knocking her cabin. Everyone predicted that Sid is making platform for his Ph.D. admission under Padmini Madam. Few of my classmates, who were toppers in earlier semesters, hated him for that. He was slowly becoming the cause which was reducing other's possibilities to get admission in Ph.D. under Padmini Madam. In fact, toppers were interested in Ph.D. for a good amount of fellowship, free residential quarters and bright future.

In that air conditioned igloo auditorium with a projector facility, we all settled with the pen drive in our pocket. I had also prepared a PowerPoint presentation of my independent research project proposal and saved it in my pen drive.

My fake shyness transformed into the real one whenever I had to face any interview, viva voce or presentation. But when I had to talk to someone, I felt less shy, like with Ravin. And also when I was completely lonely, I didn't feel any shyness. For example, in front of the bathroom mirror listening to erotic audio story in Sid's voice.

I assumed I would narrate my proposal in three minutes. Madam kept four minutes for each presentation. Sid was sitting with Padmini Madam in the first row. As presentation went on role number wise, I was becoming more and more restless.

In between, Madam and Sid kept discussing about the proposals being narrated on the projector. Sometimes Siddharth was also asking questions as if he would be a professor. Even he asked for *Bisleri* water to peon by pointing his thumb towards his mouth.

On my turn, I reached the stage with my cloud of stage fright. I kept my eyes on the projector, reading more from the slides and explained less. I was avoiding looking at anyone. Not even once. Though I had tried enough to be in good terms with Sid, I had a little fear because he was the kind of guy who could start arguing about my proposal anytime. I gave one more try to please Siddharth indirectly. I had made my proposal from the correction he found out in the method of preparation of *Coumarine* perfume. I thought it would surely result in more appreciation to Siddharth by Madam. And thereby, he would keep calm during my presentation.

My presentation was about to reach its end. Siddharth was laughing soundlessly. He pressed his lips tightly. It was difficult to understand whether he was teasing or appreciating me. But I was happy that he avoided arguing over anything. I just needed his silence. After I finished, I heard him saying something to Madam in a low voice, almost like whispering.

"My project is stronger than hers. You will like it," Sid said.

"Obviously, I am sure," Madam said.

After me, it was his turn. On the stage, he started with the confidence of some big motivational speaker.

"I want to work on any project with my beautiful lab partner, Shama," he said and dared to point his index finger towards me, proving him to be an asshole again.

"But if you ask me about my proposal, I am with a proposal for cost effective synthesis and application of *Viagra*. Yes, you heard right. *Sildenafil* molecule. I personally believe, and as we all know, erectile dysfunction can ruin a sex life and thereby our expensively made life. It is very important to have all our manly weapons in working conditions. What do you say, Shama?"

Without waiting for any response, he clicked on the keyboard for showing the first slide of his project.

After a stunned silence of ten seconds, everyone had their stomach muscles dilated due to laughter.

"Shut up," suddenly Padmini Madam screamed and the hullabaloo of laughter drowned off inside all the stomachs.

Even though few students weren't able to control their laughing whosoever's eyes caught a light background on Sid's presentation slide on the projector. It was a picture of "before and after". *"Before Viagra"* was the sleeping weapon of man. *"After Viagra"* it was erect.

I hoped that he was regretting all that he did just now. But very soon, I found myself wrong. Actually, his teasing smile and proud eyes were saying he was extremely happy with his proposal.

Everyone's laughter at me, forced me to cry. I covered my face with both hands and tears started falling. My initial silent crying gradually converted to something like moaning. Firstly, my classmates seated next to me, noticed me and became serious and then, after a little while, others also. I made that moment more intense than it was.

"Stop your slide show," Madam breathed deeply and roared to Sid.

"But Madam, I had a very interesting…"

"Bring out your pen drive now." She ordered in such an authoritative voice which couldn't be ignored. That sentence created an adverse effect on us. Those, who hadn't yet seen "before & after" picture, now found it out there. They whispered in the ears of their neighbors so that they didn't miss it.

"Just let me finish my presentation, Madam. I told you I have a far better proposal than Shama," said Sid.

In spite of that serious atmosphere, he kept mentioning my name. My crying tone kept increasing so much so that even Madam recognized it. She came to me and hugged me tightly. "Stop it, Shama. Stop now," she said.

She went on the stage, brought out his pen drive, and threw it towards the gate.

"Get out before I slap you," she said in a graver voice. Undeniable. I loved her words. The air conditioner failed to keep our auditorium's temperature low.

Sid stormed out of the auditorium, ranting a lecture.

"Don't encourage *Viagra* research. Keep yourself unsatisfied and crying all the time. And then throw that anger in man's mind for whole life. That's what stupid women have done so far. The whole department is behaving as if gender is everything. If there is a problem inside the underwear, we have to put it off. We, chemists have to understand chemistry there," said Siddharth.

He valued my tears to zero. His style was directly challenging the power of Padmini Madam as a professor and her reputation as a real researcher who had been provided a personal lab for her research by UGC.

Sid picked up his pen drive from the floor and finally moved out. His competitors for Ph.D. admission under Madam, felt a great relief. He had left the race on his own.

Now, looking back, I am thinking that if Madam would have a little prediction about the future, would she behave the same way?

6.

My two weeks had passed with relief, at least in the classroom. Siddharth had been coming every day before Shardul Sir's lecture to put his bag on the first bench and left.

Whenever we came across each other, we tried to ignore each other like kids, who are angry and not in talking to each other deliberately.

Once I told one of the girls in my class to ask him why he was keeping his bag in the classroom every day.

"For attendance," he answered. "The presence of my bag here proves I came into the classroom, but left due to punishment. So, Shardul Sir may not consider me as absent."

He smiled and went on so loudly that I could hear.

"Now say this to that girl with whom you are sitting on the first bench every day," Sid said and that girl found herself in between mine and Sid's scathing glances.

I couldn't get how he came to know that I had sent that girl to ask him. I wanted to ask Sid about that because when I was requesting my neighbor girl for that help, no one was there.

After finishing punishment of staying away from Shardul Sir's lecture for two weeks, that day, Sid was going to join again. We all were expecting a scene again. I and my neighbor girl had changed our place to last bench in a girl's column in advance. I had already grabbed useless attention because of being a part of Sid's last scene in our igloo auditorium.

"Sir, may I . . ?" Sid knocked the door after prayer "*Hamko man ki shakti dena, Man vijay kare.*"

"Yes," Shardul Sir said. "Bring your body inside."

His level of bad English brought a smile on Siddharth's face. His lips were reddish than normal as if he would have eaten *kala khatta* ice *gola* just before.

"Who painted your face such a red?" Sir asked.

"It's because I ate something." The red juice droplets almost dripped out of his mouth as he spoke.

"What is this something?"

"Dried *Nicotiana tabacum*, crushed areca nuts & saffron blended scented solid, hugged by green betel leaf, layered with one is to one mixture of lime and water."

After a silence of half minute, Sid said, "Sorry Sir. I employed Medicinal chemistry terms for the something I ate. It was just *paan*. *Qimam bahar* one thirty-five."

As expected, the scene had begun. He spoke so fluently as if he was using that description of *paan* every day. Sid's fan club, which was formed recently, roared with laughter. It reminded me of my breakdown which had happened among these uncontrollably laughing classmates in the auditorium.

"Haven't you read anywhere that chewing tobacco is injurious to health?" said Sir.

I am sure that Sir spoke that sentence rightly because he hadn't composed it.

"But Sir, what if someone doesn't want to be healthy? Nothing Sir," Sid said without waiting for any answer. "I just swore to my mother yesterday that I will not smoke now onwards. Therefore, I just started trying *paan*. In fact, I like to absorb any form of tobacco."

"Statue the chewing *paan*, disappear yourself from here, delete reddish paint and then come," Sir ordered.

"Sir, I just came to ask you if you may extend my punishment. I mean I don't want to attend these Medicinal chemistry lectures for whole semester. Is it possible?" Sid said.

"But why, man?"

"I don't think this subject needs any teaching. Not for me."

"Ok, then leave now. Don't waste other's clock."

"Other's clock? Oh… ok ok. Other's time. But Sir, what about my attendance?"

"Never worry. Your role number?"

"Twenty-five, I will keep my bag always here as a proof that I came but not attended lecture due to punishment," Sid said.

He left like a winner, like a small boy just won the match and on his way to home. One girl from his fan club whispered, "*Paan khaye saiyaan hamaro.*"

Shardul Sir explained the need of teaching Medicinal chemistry for the rest of the lecture. He tried really hard, of course with English also, to prove that his teaching was perfectly necessary. I had my own reason to be happy. The absence of that dog was my happiness. Even if, it was only for one lecture.

7.

Next day, in the practical session, I was looking here and there, thinking what to do with the project. Madam hadn't yet confirmed about which project she had registered for our pair. Siddharth had already started doing some experiments in the lab about which I had no idea. As usual, he became instantly busy just after wearing the white apron and blue hand gloves. There were no lines of regret in his face for what he did yesterday in Shardul Sir's lecture. Perhaps he had no time for anything but his experiments.

Ravin came to my work space. He had an uncanny ability to whisper in such a way that no one could catch our discussion or if we were even talking. He always came, dissolved in the air of full of chemical scents, talked to me in minimum sentences and left. He gave away the clue to others to understand that I was *taken*.

"So baby, what project are you doing?" Ravin asked, his eyes fixed on my best curve.

I narrated whole scene happened in the auditorium in minimum words, in my lowest voice, avoiding hand gestures. I took care that Sid shouldn't get it at all. Ravin looked at Siddharth busying himself, for a while.

"Don't look at him," I warned him. "Can you ask Padmini Madam about which project she want me to do? Obviously she will choose my presented proposal but I should confirm her permission. What do you say?"

"Wait. Let me ask her. Is she there in her cabin?" Ravin said.

I nodded. He knocked Madam's cabin as if he was a colleague. He came out with the expected answer. I and Sid were registered to do the project which I presented.

"Actually I came here to share good news," Ravin said. "My fellowship is revised as per new UGC guideline- Eighteen thousand five hundred rupees. I believe your kiss was my lucky charm. My astrologer also confirmed that." He left with that last sentence.

I decided to take advantage of being in the sympathetic zone of Padmini Madam. Yes. As soon as possible! I saw Siddharth was carefully weighing some solid chemical powders on micro balance. Being sure that he was not noticing me, I knocked the door of Madam's cabin for the first time.

"Yours yours. Your project, Shama. You both are registered for it. All the best," she said hurriedly, putting off her frameless spectacles.

"May I come in, Madam?" I exhaled chemicals vapors, breathed in the air-conditioned atmosphere.

She was looking so busy on her laptop that I doubted whether she remembered me as a member of her sympathetic zone or not.

"I hope you remember what happened with me yesterday," I said, trying to make my eyes teary but I failed.

"Yes Shama. Try to forget it. Start focusing on your project," she said. She fixed her eyes on the laptop again.

"Sure Madam. But I request you to punish him- my disgusting lab partner!"

"I have already punished him by choosing your proposal instead of his."

"Madam, what is the punishment in this?" I argued.

"I haven't allowed him to do the project he wanted. It's real punishment, Shama. You don't know the pain of research hungry minds because you are not one. People like me and Siddharth can really feel punished when we couldn't satisfy our research curiosity," said Madam. I couldn't get whether she was punishing him or insulting me, perhaps both.

"I am also interested in research, Madam," I said and that sentence didn't sound apt enough from my mouth. She smiled at me.

"You have proposed the project based on Siddharth's findings. What is your own idea? I think you have no idea," she said. I started looking down as she went on.

"It will be better for you to do the same project. When Siddharth is with you as a lab partner, there will be no problem. And you know? He emailed me his project which I stopped him to narrate. It shocked me now. No. Not the way you are thinking. Honestly, I assure that he is bigger scientist than his age," she said, looking up at me from her laptop.

I couldn't compose any sentence to argue back.

"I too was in the lookout for boys when I was in your age," she said.

I predicted from her face which seemed full of regrets and blushes, that she had chosen the wrong boy. The boy who was in need of *Viagra* but not allowed to it for some reasons. Siddharth mentioned such a project and touched the wrong nerve in her which possibly resulted in that anger of Madam. (How could such a suspicious thought came in my mind? Now I can figure out that Siddharth's erotic audio story was the source of my thinking.)

Everyone knew that Padmini Madam couldn't be angry just because of that kind of proposal he presented. In fact, in the previous semester, she already taught us about the science of love and role of testosterone, oestrogen, adrenaline, dopamine, serotonin, oxytocin and vasopressin without any hesitation. She even asked us if anyone has difficulty in understanding it.

I had come out of her cabin and sympathetic zone, very quickly and simultaneously.

I passed by Siddharth, who was still weighing on micro balance. Without looking at me, he said, "So how was it?"

"Madam told me that we should start experiments for the proposal I presented," I said in a requesting tone. There was no point to show him my disappointment.

"No no. Not that," he said looking at me, "How it was when you had covered your face with scarf, left hostel at 6 pm and came back at 8 pm?"

I pretended to look normal but inside me, an earthquake exploded.

"This kind of investigation will not make you the CBI chief," I said.

"But this kind of experimentation and lab work will make me something," Siddharth said, penning some weight figures in his record book.

"Ok, lab partner, let's plan out for our project," I said, changing his attention from my last Sunday outing.

"Your proposal is originally my idea," he said. "Now do it yourself. If you find your mind too small for it, tell me. I never say no to my lab partner. And I will be doing my *Viagra* project secretly. Isn't it a great deal to control each other by keeping secrets? Now, better you also start the project and become something. Something better than just a beautiful foolish girl."

His teasing smile and his didactic words were not at all in accordance.

"How dare you call me fool?" The earthquake inside me was overflowing.

"I forgot it but as I saw that private bank employee kind of guy some time ago, it reminded me of you both as…"

I looked in his eyes without blinking, unbuttoned my apron and said, "Let's meet in the library and clarify things right now."

He didn't seem to follow me. He kept weighing something. He was in no hurry at all. When he moved to his work place with all weighed solid powders, "Are you coming?" I asked.

"I told you just now that I never say no to my lab partner. No matter how hot, cold, weird or fool she is. You go there, I am coming in a while."

The door of the library was slightly open. No one was there inside because it was a time of practical sessions. The librarian and peon were inside the small cabin which couldn't be seen from the table I chose. I sat on a chair near a corner which was far from the entrance. I felt there was not enough light in that corner. There was a permanent smell of old papers due to old hard bound scientific journals kept there from so many years. I had never been there. I saw hundreds of black covered, dusty journals. Soon I heard the steps of Siddharth and started listing the things in my mind which I wanted to discuss frankly with him. He sat in front of me, kept his record book and pencil on the table we were sharing.

"Super! This is a perfect place. Let me predict how you know this place. You must be meeting Ravin here. He might be coming here for referencing from these journals for his so-called research," said Sid.

"What you do is research and all others are faking it, right?"

"You tell me, what is the benefit of any of the present research in Medicinal chemistry?" he said. "Death is sure. Today or tomorrow. To reduce pain, pain killers are already invented. He and Shardul Sir are just wasting chemicals and government's fellowship. What I do is real research. *Viagra*. Hardness. Happiness. I think all scientists should focus on this one thing. You also can try to find a molecule for female. Female *Viagra*. What say?"

"Well, now let's do some important discussion."

"What else to discuss? *Viagra* research is the most important and urgent thing in science today."

"Why are you keeping an eye on me? I can go anytime, anywhere and of course with anyone. How did you know about my last Sunday with Ravin?" I said.

"Hahaha.. Haven't you read George Orwell's novel 1984? Big brother is watching you. By the way, I am the big brother of Vidyanagar," said Sid, joking on my unawareness.

"Please!" I said.

"That old gatekeeper of your hostel is my friend. At evening, he stands at your hostel and during daytime at ours. Do you remember that old atlas bicycle I was using for a week before getting admission here, it was his. I borrowed from him. I had told him to remember your timings."

"But why do you need to know? You already know I am progressing with Ravin. Isn't it?" I said, trying hard to keep my voice low.

"Yes, I like that," he said.

"What? I am not getting you. What do you like?" I asked.

"I want you to have some experience. Looking at you, I can confirm that you have never kissed anything properly other than your own shoulders and other people's children. I hate the newcomer girlfriend who doesn't know how to kiss. Last year, one girl started kissing me. I can bet she was a beginner. While kissing, her mouth took shape as if she had a big and spicy *panipuri* inside her mouth. What a waste of time it was with her. I am telling you; don't even fantasize me before learning how to kiss."

"I don't think about these kinds of things."

"You should. All good girls of our age group think about it most of their time. And some very good girls listen to my cassette regularly."

"So… you want me to learn all the science of kissing."

"No no good girl, I want you to have practical sessions of kissing, not just to settle at the theory. Don't you observe me? How seriously I work in the lab and how carelessly in the classroom. I love the people made up from experience. Be like that as soon as possible. I am waiting for you. I am the future."

I hated him for his confident words.

We heard gradually increasing voice of walking. Sid opened his record book and took out one scientific journal from the cupboard. Shardul Sir reached at the entrance.

"What are you people doing here during practical session?" said Sir.

"Sir, we are partners," Sid said.

"What?"

"Oh! I mean lab partners. We came here to find out reference for our project which is based on *Coumarin* perfume synthesis," Sid said, pointing a finger towards opened record book and hard bound journal."

"If next time, I will catch you both like that, I mean in solitude and with opposite gender quality, I will punish you to go and rotate the ground," said Sir, pointing his index finger in the direction of play ground which was behind our department.

We nodded and started walking out immediately. We had hidden a big bubble of laughter just behind our lips. Sir had been stand there only. When we passed by him, I whispered, "Sorry Sir."

Very soon, we found ourselves out of his sight. Our hidden bubble burst out.

"Oh God! Rotate the ground. Hahaha…" Sid said. "He must be speaking under water swimming as underground swimming." I laughed like never before.

"Only fools like Ravin can do research under such a language expert," said Sid.

I didn't mind his taunts on Ravin. My eyes were so full of tears like they were in the auditorium two days before. But this time,

I was not hiding my face by hands. Instead, due to laughter over my capacity, I had to take support of Siddharth's shoulder. Next moment, I found myself hanging like a necklace on his neck. His face was expressionless like the face of a comedian, after cracking his best joke. The lines of smile stayed on my face until I put on my apron again. My anger and decision, before our library meeting, had been now converted to laughter and acceptance of Sid as a lab partner. Let me conclude, I had stopped feeling any problem by his presence. That's it. Neither more nor less.

8.

We, I mean all chemistry students, wannabe M.Sc.s and Ph.D.s, had been settled in the moderately chilled igloo auditorium. We had followed the unsaid rule. We, girls and boys, minded space between us and were sitting like our arrangement in Shardul Sir's lecture. But there was some other class which was dividing us further. In the first row, Ph.D. students, then M.Sc. final students and in the farthest part from the stage, M.Sc. previous students.

More than half the strength of department, were present there and seated according to their class. There was a little chaos like murmuring before a movie in cinema. My classmate sitting next to me pinched me on my waist.

"He is coming," she said.

"Who?" I said, throwing my sight to find someone.

"Your future. Who else?" she said, pointing towards Ravin by eyes.

He was on the way towards me. As usual, he came to me to make an indirect claim on me in front of others.

"You will be in my team," said Ravin. "Ok? Don't worry."

I nodded. But, I was not worrying about anything. I didn't care about what he said. I knew it was his way for showing off that he did have some information in advance.

Two peons had been coming down from the stage after adjusting the sound and height of the mike. Now, Siddharth entered with his fan club fanning around him. He earned his fans after scenes in Shardul Sir's lecture and Padmini Madam's project pitching session in the auditorium. Those were the students who always liked hustle and bustle in regular system. But they couldn't have guts to do anything of that sort by themselves. They needed someone like him to cling onto. Sid's entry was like that of a villain in the south Indian movies. All his fans were insisting him to say something from the stage. Those, who were already sitting also joined his fan club and kept on insisting him. Siddharth didn't resist. It looked as if he was already ready to go on the stage.

Ravin and some other research students started saying, "Sir can reach anytime. It's eleven already." But their voice couldn't get noticed between that, "Sidhdhuuu…sidhdhu, Sidhdhuuu… sidhdhu."

The cute nick name had formed instantly by his original and instant fans. No one knows exactly who found it out. As Sid knocked the mike by his index finger, some enthusiasts whistled. Everyone forgot that the gathering was to hear something from Shardul Sir.

Suddenly, I felt a wave of danger hurling inside me. As I saw Siddharth on the stage, it reminded me that he could mention my name and say something funny or terrible about me as he did earlier in the same auditorium.

"I believe the right girl for me is here, in some corner of this auditorium," Siddharth said from the stage. He was pointing and rounding his index finger towards the girl's section. When he pointed exactly at me and then started using that finger to find the treasure of gold particle in his left nostril. He found one and made a gesture like throwing it in my direction. I felt my fear becoming reasonable. His fans started shouting, "Bhabhi, bhabhi…"

"But unfortunately," he said. "Our auditorium is a round igloo. See, there are no corners."

I felt like an arrow just passed by me, leaving me unhurt. I joined his fan club with a little giggle. Happily, but afraid. He was still there. Yet there were no sign of Shardul Sir.

I was sure about Siddharth's ability to extend the joke. Before he could say something, Ravin stood up and said, "Sir is about to come. Better you get down now."

"Oh thanks," he said. "You reminded me of one thing from Shardul Sir's childhood. You people want to hear?"

Everyone shouted in agreement including me. I felt relief to know that he had left me and now focusing Shardul Sir.

He wrote a word "beans" on a small white board hanged on the side and started narrating that incident.

"A teacher asked her students to use the word "beans" in a sentence."

"My father grows beans," said one girl.

"My mother cooks beans," said a boy.

A third student, whose name was Shardul, spoke up, "We are all human beans."

The igloo was now full of laughter. His instant fans converted to the original fans.

"Thank you," said Sid and announced the end of his performance. He started walking down. Almost everyone shouted, "No no… one more please."

Someone gave him an idea. "Now please tell us about Padmini Madam's childhood. Please… please."

Sid moved back to the mike.

"Last one. In her childhood, our Padmini Madam was as clever and interested in science as she is now. She was a big fan of Rajnikanth. Once her teacher asked, "How can we solve the problem of population?" Our Padmini Madam said, "If Rajnikanth may give one of his testicles as a new planet, half of the population can move there."

All boys giggled. Most of girls covered their mouths with their hands. Sid had performed up to everyone's expectations.

Suddenly, a silence of seriousness spread from the students who saw Shardul Sir, Padmini Madam and other professors coming from the entrance. Sir and Madam had noticed that Siddharth was on the stage. They looked at each other and said nothing as if there was nothing to discuss about. Perhaps, they had plans to control him. But, not for that particular time and place. They avoided all possible scenes there. Madam sat with other professors and Shardul Sir reached to the mike on the stage.

"Good morning," he started.

"Good morning Sir . . ." we said like singing.

"The NAAC committee, The National Assessment and Accreditation Council," he said, reading from a paper, "Will visit our building to investigate our *lift*."

Only M.Sc. previous year's students didn't understand him. Shardul Sir never taught in M.Sc. previous year. I perfectly understood that meaning of his word "lift" was "uplifting or progress."

Every year such a meeting had been organized before the visit of NAAC. Every year NAAC insulted our institute by awarding us "C grade".

In short, Sir wanted to say, "They are visiting our institute for periodic assessment and accreditation."

"If we will handle them with care, I am sure they will fall in love at first sight with us. Trust me they will leave us with "A grade". When you will go for any interview at companies, you can proudly pronounce. "Yes, I am from Sardar Patel University which is labeled "A grade" by NAAC." Your competitors from other universities will feel the fire from you if our university can be illuminated by "A grade" from NAAC this time. I think if we will get "A grade", all our final year students will be exploited by campus interviews only. There will be no need to knock the door of any company for bread and butter. Or ghee, whatever you want. So, we had made six teams to get prepared. Six research students will guide those teams of all final year students. Please just follow them for three days. After that, NAAC will land here for a day. Thank you for patient hearing."

Sir left the stage with pride on his fluent English.

Siddharth and I were in Ravin's team. Ravin had distributed whole work of preparation for NAAC visit. For him, to work efficiently for getting better grade from NAAC, was also a kind of buttering up Shardul Sir, his Ph.D. guide. It was just an addition to his driving duties.

Academic work had been stopped for three days. Someone had to clean exhaust fans of lab, someone had to write tags and instructions of instruments, someone had to make colorful *rangoli* at the entrance, and someone had to arrange gifts and mementos for NAAC members. I was given a soft work by Ravin. I had to dress up in the traditional *sari*, look beautiful, and keep smiling and present bouquet of flowers to NAAC members.

Ravin had instructed Sid to arrange bouquets from the flower shop. Siddharth also had to pick up NAAC members from AC coach of the train and bring them to university guest house.

Everyone did whatever they were told to do. All black boards were now clean. All practical work hoods were looking new and unused. Tattered and leaking acid room of hazardous chemicals was closed tightly. Every notice board had new notices printed on extra white papers. Rusted name plates of old faculty members, were changed to new ones. New shining glasses of drinking water were kept chained together. Two giant *Gulmohar* trees in our parking and campus area were trimmed. They were looking like a boy who just had a fresh hair cut. Our campus had put on a new glow as if it was just constructed and NAAC officers were corrupt ministers coming for its inauguration.

* * *

It was a bright cold day of January. All the faculty of the department and some of us were gathered at the decorated gate. We had written “Welcomes NAAC” under our big poster of “Department of Chemistry”. A white Baleno car arrived. Front wheel of car rolled over a beautiful *Rangoli* designed at the side of entrance gate. It messed it up.

We couldn’t believe the sight of Siddharth, smoking on the driver’s seat.

“Why did you choose that stupid?” Shardul Sir asked Ravin. He looked down.

Sid came out and opened the door of back seat. One NAAC member, fat, bored with his own weight, put one leg out of the car. Sid helped him to come out by giving a hand support. They completely ignored our presence. We were waiting there to welcome them. Officer took a deep breath. He asked for a cigarette through a finger gesture. Siddharth took out one from the upper pocket of his shirt and gave him. When he placed it in between his blackish lips, Sid offered a lighter. He accepted it and winked. Siddharth lighted his cigarette in filmy gesture. Officer kept enjoying warmth of smoking for around half minute. He avoided any movement as if he wanted to keep burnt ashes intact with cigarette. But it didn't last. Ashes had blown off with a light wind. Sid and officer smiled to each other.

"*Sirji*, try again in a closed room." We heard Siddharth's words.

Shardul Sir and we all were in shock by looking at their friendly behavior.

"I think you did right," Shardul Sir said Ravin who was yet looking down, regretting his decision of sending Sid to receive NAAC officers.

From another door of the car, one more officer came out with Harry Potter spectacles.

"This time, don't worry about grade," Padmini Madam whispered in the ear of Shardul Sir, looking at that officer. "He was my friend during my years in IIT. Not only that, he proposed me too. We ended on a good note."

That NAAC officer immediately joined hands and looked like saying *namaskar* to all of us. His eyes took little more time on Madam.

Fat officer threw the remained cigarette and chopped it by his black shoes. All the faculty members stepped ahead towards them with the words "welcome welcome" in their mouths.

Shardul Sir shook hands with fat officer and said, "How was your journey?"

"Too comfortable. Siddharth managed everything well," he answered.

"Yes yes, he is the brightest kid of our department," said Shardul Sir.

Padmini Madam welcomed her old classmate with bouquet of flowers.

"I can't accept it," he said with teasing smile. "Revenge! Why did you reject the rose I offered you?"

Both laughed. Madam threw her celebrity smile and finally he took the bouquet. They started walking towards the glass door of the department.

"What Swami?" Madam said. "You haven't changed those glasses yet? Twenty two years went. Isn't it?"

"Padmi, I changed it. But, found out this one again as I came to know that I would be visiting your department. Just to scan you again with that same sight. But *yaar*, you also haven't changed especially that smile."

Both NAAC members and some core members of our department entered in HOD's office. Shardul Sir relaxed as he realized both NAAC members seemed too happy. He predicted that the fat officer, whose name was Prof. Ashwin Hathi, would keep smoking and eating our local famous dishes (we already arranged) whole day and Swami Sir would pass the day with Padmini Madam with some dignified kind of flirting. Shardul Sir daydreamed of getting "A grade" from NAAC and thereby extending his term as the Head of the Department.

9.

We all gathered at the igloo auditorium again to have interaction session with NAAC officers. Actually there was nothing to do. Everything possible had been done already. But, we had no theory classes that day. So we all, who belonged to six working committees, were passing our time there.

I had been dressed in a maroon and white *sari*, gifted by Ravin. I was given a duty to offer a bouquet of flowers to NAAC members when interaction session would start. Ravin and me, sat on the side of the first row.

"Our department should get A grade," he said and touched my earring, looking at me. "Just because you are here in this department. My beautiful baby."

He didn't try but I felt like he wanted return gift in the form of a kiss. I had already started using my fake blushes.

"If you will remain such a beauty, remember my words, Shama, you will never need to do anything. Please be mine, *yaar*. Then, just rest and enjoy the whole life under the shadow of my tree," he said.

"Where is your tree?" I asked.

"It's just a way of expression, baby. Don't you understand poetic language?"

"I understand. But I thought shadow only happens in day time. So what will I do in the night time? Hahaha… Just kidding. Why are you pleasing me yet? Do you have any doubt? Hadn't I kissed you properly?" I said and started rearranging my green and golden bangles.

"No. No," he said. "I mean yes yes."

We both saw Siddharth coming towards me with two silvery decorated mementoes and bouquets of flowers. He had become the more important person for the event than all six research students. Yet, he was becoming bigger by doing small things he had been given to do. Before he reached to us, Ravin went away. I couldn't hear what excuse he gave for leaving me suddenly. I thought he felt jealous of Sid.

"Keep it. Two mementoes and bouquets for both of them. Right?" he said. I nodded.

"How did you manage to be so friendly with that fat officer? Or did you know him from any other connection?" I said, taking the mementoes from him.

"Will discuss stupid things later. Let's talk about the important thing we couldn't finish in that silent and dark corner of library," he said.

"What was that?" I said pretending that I really forgot it. "I forgot. Leave it whatever it was. It's not important now. Now it is more important whether department will get "A grade" or not? I am sure this time we will get it. What say?"

"Though I haven't had any personal interest in getting any grade, but as you seem too much interested in it, let's bet over that," he said.

"What bet? I mean what kind of bet?" I was expecting a weird answer from him.

"If department will get "A grade", you will kiss me. Vacuum kiss on lips at the silent corner you discovered in the library," he said. "If no "A grade", I will kiss you. What say?"

"I don't want to bet of any kind," I said. "Besides, I would rather kiss Chris Gayle over you." I started rearranging my bangles in random manner.

"There's no accounting for your tastes. But Chris Gayle is in West Indies. Too far. So, instead, you buy a leather purse and kiss it. I think you need kissing badly."

"Why do you think you are the proper person? I can get whoever I want," I said.

I really wanted someone to come near us and break the conversation.

"But what's wrong with me?" he said carelessly. "I heard I kiss too well."

The conversation was not going the way I expected. It never did when I was with him. After our meeting in library, I expected that we will remain in workable terms and I will finish this semester smoothly.

"Everyone is complementing me for my beauty in this *sari*. I hope you would also like to comment," I said, trying to divert his attention from kissing to some decent thing.

"Just this *sari* is coming in between your beauty and my eyes."

I knew he was teasing, but, as always, his teasing maddened me. There was always too much of the disturbing truth in the things he said.

"Now leave me alone. And I don't ever want to speak to you again." I stopped playing with my bangles. Two bangles overlapped and jammed with each other.

I stood up to go away. I heard he was saying, "Then, how will our project work? We are lab partners; we can't get away from each other. We aren't husband-wife, who can leave other anytime. Isn't it? O hello…"

10.

As Shardul Sir expected, Prof. Hathi was enjoying our prearranged local food in HOD's office and Swami was in her Padmi Madam's cabin. They spent the entire day like that. Just before an hour of interaction session, they demanded to visit some sections of the department against Shardul Sir's expectations.

"We have to submit our report to UGC. It's our duty," Hathi said and licked his fingers over tongue. All the dishes were emptied now. Ash tray was full. He adjusted his belt and kept his file under his shoulder.

"One spent the whole day digesting and inhaling carbon dioxide and nicotine, another is playing with old unbaked romance in closed cabin. And now these bastards suddenly remembered their duties," Shardul Sir said to himself. He was too much disturbed by imagining Padmi and Swami together in her closed cabin.

Hathi and Swami visited almost each corner of the department. Swami captured some photos and Hathi kept writing something in his file after reviewing places like library, lab, acid room, instrument wing, classrooms and some so-called research labs.

“Why does everything look over-cleaned?” Swami said. “Seems like no one is using anything here.”

No one answered him.

Shardul Sir thought, “If it is clean, they doubt we are doing nothing, if messed up with chemicals, they want cleanliness. Oh god! What do they want on earth?”

“Our discussion session begins at 4.30 and all students have already reached there. So, shall we move now?” Shardul Sir tried this sentence twice but Hathi and Swami ignored it.

Without any apparent reason, they became dutiful officers of UGC. They remembered their responsibilities after satisfying desires of senses. Hathi was done with desires of smell of smoking and taste of food. Perhaps Swami was done with softer desires of sight, touch, and hearing in Madam’s cabin.

“We regret we couldn’t see everything,” they said later at 5:20 pm. “But, it’s enough. Let’s move in the auditorium.”

In spite of sitting comfortably in the 24°C air conditioned and fresh lush green sprinkled air of igloo, everyone was bored of waiting. We were there from around one hour. We got so bored of waiting that fan club had started convincing Siddharth to go on the stage. But, he refused.

“We had seriously spent three days to work on making better appearance of the department,” Siddharth said. “I can’t take risk for few minutes of fun. Let’s first get “A grade” from NAAC, after that, we will again become like our original grade. Which is Z-.”

All cheered up shamelessly. He promised to perform in "Today's education: In my sight" oratory held after two weeks and made his fan club happy.

On the stage, there were three chairs behind a decorated table. Three tags were labeled for one HOD and two NAAC members. Hathi, Swami and Shardul Sir took their seats. Hathi tried and succeed to fit in the chair. Padmini Madam located herself in the first raw in audience, exactly in front of her beloved Swami Sir. She had a kind of confidence on his face as if she would about to become a major reason for getting "A grade" accreditation. She had blinked eyes to Shardul Sir as an indication of saying that, "Feel free. "A grade" is almost confirmed. I have performed too well in my closed cabin."

We all stood up to show our respect. We sat down as they indicated us to take our seats.

"I welcome Prof. Hathi Sir and Prof. Swami Sir on the behalf of our department," Ravin announced from the mike. "We can easily see lines of satisfaction on the face of both of you, Sir. I hope you really liked our department in every way of judgment. Now, I request Miss Shama to present a bouquet and the memento to Hathi Sir."

I was already ready at the corner of the stage. I reached to Hathi Sir and threw my smile all over. I can say that my smile was a strong competitor of that of Padmini Madam. And then I presented a bouquet to Swami Sir also. My role in NAAC visit finished with that. They both thanked and kept their bouquets and mementos on the table.

"Now let's start interaction session," Ravin went on. "I hope you all will take part gracefully. Swami Sir, please hold the mike now."

Before Swami Sir would start any discussion, Sid reached the stage and took both bouquets from the table. Everyone was astonished and my classmates confirmed in their minds that "another scene has begun."

"What happened, Sid? Keep it there and take your seat." Shardul Sir said in a requesting tone.

"I committed to gift shop owner that I will return these bouquets to him as such at 5.45 evening. I brought it on rent, Sir. My working team leader informed me that NAAC officers are big named professors. They will not take it with them. So, let me reach the gift shop on time. And I am not at all responsible for this late start of interaction session. Am I?"

Shardul Sir couldn't believe what he heard. And we did too. It took time to get it.

"Sid, why are you making stories?" said Shardul Sir. There was no gentleness in his voice now.

"See this bill of rent, Sir," Sid took out a pink slip from his pocket. "If you don't believe me, let's call the number on the bill. We will put the phone on speaker if you wish."

"Siddharth," Swami interfered. "You can leave with both bouquets. Is there anymore thing you want to say?"

"Yes," Sid said. "Acid room of hazardous chemicals is totally air packed which isn't a proper and safe practice. But as our department has just one acid room, we kept all hazardous solvents together there. It's dangerous to keep them together more than two hours. We already passed that time limit. I don't think "A grade" is more important than our health and lives."

"Shardul," Hathi said in hurried and worried voice, "Send some peons immediately to acid room."

He followed instruction and sent two peons who were

peacefully enjoying conditioned air of igloo. They left making bad faces.

Shardul Sir had suddenly acquired the look of the captain of a losing team. He tried to find better words but ended up saying to Hathi Sir, "He is a little mischievous boy."

"But in the morning, you told he is a bright student. Isn't it?" Hathi said.

Shardul Sir looked at Sid and said, "You may go now."

The dream of "A grade" became out of possibility. Most of us started hating Sid. And I already hated him for his latest fight with me.

Padmini Madam lost her celebrity smile which she was continuously throwing to Swami Sir.

I am sure if Ravin would be near to Shardul Sir, he would repeat what he said in morning, "Why did you choose that stupid?"

"Haven't I told you? They have made everything nice just for a show. This department is not at all as it seems," Swami said to Hathi. We all heard because one flexible mike was there on the table.

"Hey! You boy! Wait," Hathi said. "We visited so many institutes for accreditation. Most of them do the things which you people did. No one ever opened up things like that. What do you intent to do?"

"Sir, in the morning, we both smoked in front of everyone in our campus. Notice board of "no smoking" was exactly in front us. No one opposed. Isn't it? Whole day our department kept buttering up to you both. You hadn't started evaluation on time. I am sure no one would have said anything to you about it. We just want "A grade" on paper and want to stay with our original "Z grade" level genuinely. I believe, up to when, we will become "A grade" institute in true sense, we will keep getting poor grades every year. Decoration, cleanliness and buttering up will never help. It never did. This department has been trying these things from so many years," Siddharth said.

Everyone knew he said the complete truth. Even he dared to do personal attack on Hathi Sir. Hathi Sir had started his efforts to come out of his fitted chair. He stood up and said, "I will recommend UGC for "A grade" for this department surely. I am giving "A grade" in advance. This department has at least one student who knows how to be better. Siddharth, please tell everyone here what you think."

Sid reached to the mike, engrossing total control of the event.

"We can become "A grade" institute only if we accept our original grade. Sadly, it is Z. If patient don't believe he is sick, no one can cure him. Actually, the moment we accept we are "Z grade", immediately, journey towards "A grade" starts. No institute can stay happy with "Z" if the institute is really interested in education."

Sid's fan club couldn't stop clapping and whistling in agreement with Sid.

After NAAC members leaved, some of Sid's enthusiastic fans took Sid on shoulders as if he was a groom. He fully enjoyed the attention. When shoulders of his fans started aching and dance felt enough, they got him down. Shardul Sir came to him and hugged tightly. He couldn't say a word. He took out the pink slip of the gift shop from Sid's pocket and sent a peon with bouquets to return it. Padmini Madam showed thumbs up indication from distance to Sid. Her celebrity smile had come back on her lips. This way, she confirmed *Viagra* incident would not matter anymore.

11.

Next day, Sid sat on the first bench to attend Shardul Sir's lecture. We all thought he would be now in good terms with Sir. After prayer, Sir said, "Good good. You are back in my lecture."

"Sir, before a week, you had announced that there would be a quiz today. So, I am here for quiz. Please don't confuse. I have no intention to attend any lecture," said Sid.

I couldn't understand how he knew that Sir had announced a quiz. Sid never attended lectures. He never asked to anyone what was going on in lectures and he never had any interest in theory classes. Most of us were not prepared for quiz. We didn't like that he reminded Sir about quiz.

Sir smiled to Sid and started writing question paper on the black board. It was a short quiz and duration was ten minutes. Sid submitted his answer sheet at tenth minute and left. He kept his bag there itself on the first bench.

Sir avoided arguing with him. Perhaps Sir was only interested in "A-grade" and his extension for one more term as HOD.

In the practical session, Sid was in hurry as usual and he was putting on the apron. I couldn't stop myself from getting in talking terms back with him. He was now like a small celebrity of the campus and I was his proud lab partner.

"Hey Sid," I said, "Congratulations, you are the one and only reason for our A grade."

"Yet we haven't awarded any official notification of A grade. I think you are really serious about our bet of A grade. Bet of kissing! Believe me you need to be kissed as soon as possible," he said.

He reminded me of his stupid bet of kissing with me. I realized his old teasing mood had come back.

"So now what to do about our project? I mean *Coumarin* perfume project," I said and tried to change the topic.

Before he said anything, Padmini Madam emerged from her cabin and said, "Siddharth, meet me with your project about which you emailed me."

"Sure Madam, coming," said Sid.

"*Viagra* project will be on, I think." He told me while going.

I wished that would not turn into reality. I wanted him to work with me for perfume project. After all it was his idea which I presented as mine. I had only presented it with little modification. Honestly, I was not able to work alone on that.

He came out of her cabin after two hours.

"She just wanted to know more about my *Viagra* proposal. But for this semester, we both are registered for *Coumarine* perfume project," he said.

Now, doors of Madam's cabin had been opened for Sid. He was spending a lot of time there discussing about his proposal, referencing some online literature on Madam's computer. He just came out sometimes and kept instructing me about our perfume project. Past toppers of my class again started thinking that he would get Ph.D. admission in Padmini Madam's lab. He really became a strong competitor for Ph.D. admission seekers.

When Shardul Sir distributed answer sheets of our quiz, we all were surprised. Sidharth got full marks even though he never attended Sir's lecture.

12.

After a week, everyone looked at the notice board. There was a copy of official notification from NAAC. UGC awarded our department the same grade as every year- "C" grade.

It seriously affected Shardul Sir's walking pattern. He started walking too slowly like Hathi Sir, depressed with his weight. In lecture also, he distributed Xerox copies of the unit he wanted to teach. He avoided taking pain of writing on the black board.

Padmini Madam felt cheated as if she has paid proper price and doesn't get the thing, decided with Swami Sir, inside her closed cabin. She always wanted that the department must have "A grade" from NAAC. After all she was a proud IITian. She had cleared UGC-NET for six consecutive years. How could she like to belong to any "C grade" department? Her disappointment seemed as clear as her celebrity smile which was lost now. She stopped inviting Sid to her cabin. "Better you focus on your perfume project. This is final semester," she said to Sid in plain voice, keeping her eyes on computer.

No one understood what to say to Siddharth. Of course, he had become the one and only factor in the decision of UGC.

I saw Sid near the notice board. He was reading the notification of C grade. He jumped as he saw me entering the department. Anyone from our department could predict that he might have read the notice saying "A grade" award from NAAC. But no, he was happy for another reason. I would say it a silly reason.

"So now, the department hasn't got the "A" grade," he said. "Do you remember our bet? I have to kiss you now. Vacuum kiss on lips at the silent corner you discovered in the library. Hahaha. Let's move there."

He told with wetting and softly touching his upper lip by tongue. It was as dirty as his audio story in cassette.

"As per your strong suggestion, I am practicing kissing practically with Ravin," I said.

"Good good, then show me how much have you learnt? Let's move at our place."

"First let me ask you questions which were left out?" I said.

"Oh! You are such a talkative. And I never liked conversations. I am a man of action. One should suck mango if one is hungry or thirsty, instead of discussing about mangoes. Isn't it?" He again made a dirty gesture while mentioning mango.

He waited for answer. I said nothing. He went on, "Well, whatever, But I am very happy today."

"You should be ashamed of yourself. We got "C" grade and you are happy," I said.

"Oh! Please leave that A B C D now. I am happy for you."

"For me? How?" I said.

"How fast have you changed? Before some days, you were so shy that you couldn't see continuously in my thirsty eyes. And now! Now we are discussing about vacuum kissing. You have found the dark corner also."

"You are making stories yourself and befooling yourself to look happy. I haven't discussed any such things with you ever," I said.

"I don't think there's any harm in being happy. I am so happy for you that I want to gift this."

He gave me a new cassette labeled as "LISTEN ONLY, WHEN YOU ARE LONELY (2)."

It reminded me his earlier dirty audio story. I tried to give it back before anyone could spot me with it. But he didn't take it. I put it hurriedly inside my bag and confirmed that no one had noticed me.

"It's a sequel of earlier one. You will love it," he said.

"Why do you do such cheap things? I mean what do you get by all this?" I asked.

"Money. I want to stay on my own forever. By the way, I had bought my bike from my earning. And this kind of entertainment is an innocent joy in demand. No harm in it. You never heard? No work is big or small. As I told you, I am a man of action. I don't just keep speaking - Earn while you learn and all other similar sayings," he said proudly.

"How much do you earn?"

"You will know only when you play this cassette. Our budget is too much increased this time. We involved high-tech sound design in audio story- moaning, some male-female foreplay conversation, sound of rain etc. You just listen and then say.

Last time my producer sold twenty-four thousand cassettes in Gujarat. This time we hope it will cross one lakh."

"Please Sid!" I said. "Let's go to the library, you can kiss me once, yes ok vacuum kiss. But, please don't interfere when my parents would come here to meet Ravin. I am going to invite them around next week. I know you have a network. You are that big brother of Orwell's novel "1984" who is watching everyone in Vidyanagar. I can't hide anything from you. But, I am seriously progressing with Ravin. Please remember that my dad had two heart attacks."

"Why would I interfere?" he said hurriedly, "I don't want to marry you or anyone. I am not at all any kind of marriage material. Ok? Happy? Now make me happy. Let's go to library."

"How can you think that our kissing is ok thing as I am going to marry Ravin?" I asked.

"I heard marriage is a connection of souls. Then, I would say lips have nothing to do anything with marriage. One can rub lips anywhere," he said.

"You have heard lots of crap. Will you allow your wife to kiss anyone? Just anyone on earth?"

"Your memory span is really tiny. I told you just now that I am not a marriage material," he said. "Now, will you please come to library? Or did you forget that too?"

He started walking so fast towards library as if there would be burning fire there. I followed him. I don't know why but I had a kind of confidence that if I would pay him a price, he would stand on what he guaranteed. I just wanted to keep him away from my parent's meeting with Ravin. I had decided to enjoy under the shadow of Ravin's tree.

In the dark corner of library, I closed my eyes, and tried to control my heartbeats. I smelled Sid. It was his original smell. No perfume or body spray he used. He came nearer. He took my face in his hands. He kissed so gently on my left cheek that for a moment I felt as if a butterfly would have landed there. And then, it did fly away as fast as it landed. His hands had left my face.

"The price of your lip lock is so low that I do not want to buy it," he said and went away. He left me to introspect I think.

If he would have done what I agreed for, if he would have kissed me, perhaps I would have forgotten it sooner or little later. But, he had insulted my beauty, my weapon, my life mantra. I told myself, "Be happy, you got what you want without paying anything. He will not interfere in our mission to get into the shadow of Ravin's tree. Forget Sid."

The moment I decided to forget him, my mind focused on what to not remember. It was Sid. It was he whom I should not remember. I sat down, resting my head on the table for two hours. The librarian awakened me and I reached hostel with fever and four tablets of *paracetamol*.

13.

It was Saturday night. I was trying to sleep inside my quilt with my feverish and apathetic body. Paracetamol hadn't yet started working. I heard a familiar shout of "Shama two zero eight, phone…" from our hostel's common land line phone. My mother never failed to call me every alternate Saturday night.

"I will call her tomorrow," I said to the girl, who shouted my name. "Just say that. She is my mother."

I felt headache also. I took another half tablet. I requested my roommate girl to switch off the lights. I covered myself fully with a white quilt.

I saw an image of a girl. She stood at my place in the lab. She had worn my white apron with one rupees coin sized buttons. She was cooking noodles with fire in frying pan. I couldn't see her face. She had sat pan on burner at my lab work place. When second time, she tried to fire in the pan, she made a mistake. Perhaps, she added too much liquid or something other than liquid which was inflammable. Suddenly she had been exposed to the blasting fire on the pan. She was late to throw burning pan away. Her hairs on forehead, eyebrow and eyelashes had come to direct contact with flames. They burnt and instantly became randomly curly. Her nostrils filled up with unpleasant burning smell and fumes.

I found myself in the beauty parlor. I waited for my turn. The big revolving chair in front of mirror was empty. A new beautician was telling me to sit there. But, I rejected her offer and blew on my painted nails. I wanted to be handled by my regular beautician middle aged lady. "I will wait for my turn with you," I said to that lady whom I knew. They both looked at each other and smiled. I couldn't understand but I didn't ask. I kept reading cosmopolitan and comparing myself with the model's pictures. When I am done with steaming, bleaching and eyebrow, I reviewed my face and I felt something terribly missing. But I couldn't find it initially. That old lady looked at my dissatisfaction and said, "Whatever effort I do, I can't straighten your eyebrow hairs. See they are curled as if exposed to fire. Isn't it?" And she was right. I had no words to deny her opinion. It became difficult to keep looking at the mirror. I ran away. I had to run away from my reflection.

I entered my classroom with black goggles to hide my burnt eyebrows. But I had to remove goggles when Shardul Sir told me, "This is classroom, not a fashion ramp."

I wanted to cry but tears didn't come. I felt like a lump inside my throat and it wasn't moving inside or outside. I caught my throat with my whole muscle energy. My eyes got a reddish tinge. I ran away to my hostel. The gatekeeper of my hostel also didn't recognize me. He asked for my identity card. It seemed like I had become a stranger object for others and to me too. Without beauty, my identity was also lost. I regretted for going to the hostel. I wasn't able to show my face to anyone there. I decided to eat alone in any restaurant instead of the mess at my hostel. I had to call several times to the waiter to order something, unlike my previous days when waiters had been serving me on my first call. After a distasteful dinner, when I stopped an auto-rickshaw, no boys tried to sit beside me. The driver of the rickshaw stopped it at my hostel with such a halt that I bumped out of it and everyone started laughing at me.

Absence of my identity touched almost every aspect of my routine life.

It was a nightmare. I woke up at 3 am. My whole back side was wet by perspiration. Paracetamol had worked and my temperature was normal. But, I found myself under the permanent state of emergency. Every mirror became my most hated thing even though I knew it was just a dream. I told myself, "How will I face the day?"

I concluded that the dream was composed of one latest hazy memory, my fear of losing beauty and my imagination of making noodles in my future home with Ravin. During composition of dream, my mind had used a setting of my real lab work place. Last weekend, I had eaten veg-hakka noodles from a street food stall. There was nothing much to do until my order got served. So, I and most of the people around were looking at the girl cooking noodles evoking the fire on the frying pan.

* * *

In the new, clean, soft sunlight of winter morning, everything seems not just normal but delightful. I blamed only myself for taking unnecessary things seriously. I laughed on my question, "How will I face the day?"

The day was too friendly and caring. My roommate girl brought bun butter and tea for me as she was aware of my health. I thanked her. She suggested me to put an ice cube on the inner corner of my swollen eyes. Two little lakes had formed below my eyes. During breakfast, I thought that the morning time is the best time to take some action. I got fresh, went out and called my mother from a yellow STD booth. I invited my parents to visit me and Ravin as early as possible on which she agreed instantly.

I went to the department. I passed by Shardul Sir's research lab to meet Ravin. It was our secret indication for meeting. But, I never used it. Actually the need to use it was never happened. Ravin spotted me. After few minutes, we met at the dark corner of library. It was reminding me of earlier day's event with Sid at the same corner. But I hadn't given any attention. I accomplished for what I went there.

"Ravin," I said. "My parents are going to come here to check how big and comfortable your tree's shadow is."

"With poetic words, you are looking like a poem, baby," he said with exaggerated politeness. "I am excited to meet them."

He upheld my hairs and touched my earrings. He checked around to confirm that no eyes are watching us. He hugged me for around fifteen seconds.

"Have you seen notice board? "C" grade again. The whole filmy drama by that boy is responsible. What did you say?" During the hug, Ravin was talking about that A B C D. He didn't utter a word about my swollen eyes. I doubt whether he had even noticed it or not.

"I want to forget all that, *yaar*," I said. Neither he had asked nor had I told him about what I wanted to forget.

14.

At evening, I visited the beauty parlor. I felt better when I found no new beautician girl there unlike my nightmare. The middle aged lady greeted me sweetly as always, "Hey upcoming model!!" She was alone. I didn't need to wait for my turn. After threading my eyebrows, cleaning, steaming and bleaching my face, she told, "When my parlor will become a grand success like Jawed Habib, I will use your pictures as a model for advertisement."

I smiled and said, "I will always be available free of cost for you, auntie."

I left with my balloon filled fully with pride of beauty.

After getting "C" grade, atmosphere in practical sessions was also changed. I felt it as if Padmini Madam's disappointment would be spread in the lab from her cabin.

Once she came out of her cabin without the celebrity smile and said, "I can't invite any of my executive friends from big R&D companies to conduct campus interview here, in such a "C grade" department. So, do whatever you want to do in the lab. Just don't make any noise or I will detain the whole batch."

She closed her cabin's door with such impact as if she would keep it closed forever. There was no time pass chatting continued in the lab. Only a voice of exhaust fans and little sound of glassware handling remained to entertain our ears.

I would not say it as just ignoring but it was deeper than that. Sid had left teasing me after our library incident. In the lab, he told me, "I will do our perfume project alone. You can copy readings from my record book. You don't need to do anything. Whenever Madam will reach our work place, pretend as you are doing some experiments. That's it. Now, don't disturb me for anything."

I saw him doing *Viagra* synthesis experiments also. It seemed as if he had forgotten my presence. He was the busiest and the most silent one among our batch. Now the only problem remained with me was boredom. I kept reminding my earlier days of teasing, joking and pointless chit chats during lab time.

Within just two days, I reached to the stage of such a boredom that I thought to say him, "Siddharth, please. I don't say you to let me handle the project. But, at least give me some labor work of our experiments. You do quality work. I can't stay idle all the time in lab."

Yes. I would have used his registered name, written in Roll call register. "Siddharth" Our relations would not have let me use his nick name. "Sid." The name, which was in use by his big fan club.

But before I decided anything, the day of our first internal practical exam came. I just informed Ravin about my timetable of practical exam. He understood. He was present there as a supervisor with his private bank employee look without a tie.

It became easier to see an understanding and caring husband in him. But, when I was given my experiment, I felt I didn't need his help. I got the simplest exercise to perform practically. Ravin observed me doing it perfectly. Our exam duration was 4 hours. We had an optional break of ten minutes at 2.30 pm. I took it. I told Ravin, "Don't keep rounding around me in the lab. My experiment is so easy."

He agreed.

I had done every step of experiment on time. In the last half an hour, I started to do the final step. I exactly measured 150 ml solvent called *Dimethylformamide*. I poured it in the yellow reaction mass. In around two seconds, big blast with cracking noise roared from it. It seemed like flambeau in the middle of the lab. My eyes closed for a while itself. A piece of yellow mass flied and stuck to my elbow. My face exposed to fire for a fraction of second. I immediately stepped back and fell down. Everyone saw me and fire at my working hood. But, only Ravin was the one who ran first towards me. By then, Sid had opened fire extinguisher which was installed before few days as a part of preparation for NAAC visit. Fortunately it was in working condition. He extinguished the fire skillfully.

Padmini Madam could only see last fifteen seconds of fire. I started crying. Partly it was due to the damage in my beautiful face and partly to save myself from punishment by Madam. Before the start of exam, Madam had informed us about it.

"If any incident will happen, the responsible one will be detained. He or she will have to score double passing marks from the second internal exam."

I expected that Madam will ask me whether I need any first aid or not?

"What is your roll number, Shama?" Madam asked me with plain face.

Before I said anything, Ravin said, "It's my fault, Madam. I provided her *Ether* instead of *Dimethylformamide* by mistake."

Sid hung the fire extinguisher bottle on the side.

"Why are you protecting her? Sid said. "She is just a candidate appearing in her exam. She is not your sister or wife yet."

Ravin looked at Madam in the hope of angry response to Sid's comments. But, she didn't respond anything but yawning.

"Madam," Sid said. "It is possible that Ravin may have made mistake. But you see Shama had used my chemical. Let me show you that all my glass wares are labeled by my name as per our laboratory rule. She hadn't labeled any of her. She mistakenly took my *Chloroform* solvent. Look at the empty beaker of mine. As we know, *Chloroform* and her experiment's yellow reaction mass can react and result in blast only."

"No Madam, I had used the solvent provided by Ravin only." I said, keeping crying and showing off my pain.

"I haven't asked what happened and how and by whom?" Madam said. "I asked your roll number only."

"Twenty four" Sid said. "Her number is twenty four."

Madam went to her cabin. In those last twenty five minutes of exam, everyone including Sid, got busy in completing their experiments except me. I was detained.

Though I had been detained, that day cleared a lot of things for me. Who did try to save me from detention? Who did stand against me? And both of them, Sid and Ravin, stood face to face for the first time when I had been at the centre of matter.

I left the lab without waiting for end of our exam. It was over for me earlier than all. I reached hostel with some life decisions and little burning and irritating skin on the nose.

By the evening, I felt to consult doctor because irritation persisted. I kept scratching my nose with my nails for long time. It made light bruises there. I hated to see the presence of black spots on my comely shaped nose. I thought if my middle aged beautician auntie would see me now, she couldn't address me by "Hey upcoming model!" I think that thought had irritated me more than physical irritation on my nose.

My latest nightmare of losing beauty had tried to become reality. A doctor of our university health centre said after checking me, "Apply this cream at every six hours interval. It's just a matter of two or three days. You will have a fresh skin there shortly. Take a leave from college, rest, pass the time and don't scratch it."

I strictly followed his instructions. I sat an alarm for every six hours gap to remind me for applying the cream. On the morning of fourth day, my mirror confirmed me that I had defeated all the efforts of the nightmare of losing my beauty, from becoming reality.

15.

At early morning, I saw from my third floor room's window at the reception of the hostel. My parents were paying money to an auto-rickshaw driver. I hurriedly threw last sight on mirror to reconfirm that my skin had been healed well after lab incident. They showed their identity cards to the gate keeper. Yes. That gatekeeper friend of Sid, who had once given his bicycle to him. He allowed my parents to enter.

My mom had her luggage full of their clothes, valuables and a lot of dry breakfast for me. My father, with empty hands, was walking slowly with heavy steps which had a wait of third and final heart attack. Though my mother wanted to walk fast to see me as soon as possible, she had to slow down her speed to be with my father. But when they reached my room, they seemed perfectly perfect parents.

We three met and laughed on remembering my happy and comfortable childhood. Our eyes became wet by predicting near future when my father would not be with us. And then, as per my mother's suggestion, we decided to focus on present, I mean on our meeting with Ravin.

I informed them almost everything about Ravin. His fellowship, future of people having Ph.D.(Chemistry) degree, his family background and how kind he is. My mother asked me so many times in between whenever I missed any detail. After all my narration about Ravin, she felt so good that she kissed my forehead. She started looking like a proud mother who had advised her daughter rightly from years and thereby that daughter would have found happiness.

But my father? He just kept listening with plain face. He didn't utter a word during or after my talk as if he would not have anything to do with my future. But, it was the unavoidable truth we all were avoiding to mention. My mother had been disturbed by my dad's silence more than me. She told him in her low gentle voice, "Please, say something."

"I was waiting for Shama to complete her talk. Are you done, *beta*?" he said.

"I think I have told everything which I think is important," I said confidently.

"Shama, you are talking from last one hour. You are a final year postgraduate student. You haven't spoken a word about your study. Why?" he asked.

"Oh Dad, yes, my study is going well."

I told with much confidence as I was quite sure that they couldn't have information of my detention from practical exam.

"I don't know what you and your mother had been talking every alternate Saturday, but I remember what I told you. I told you to make a life. Instead I am watching you are more interested to just connect with someone's good future."

"But, I love him, Dad. You please meet him and then judge me," I said.

"Ok *beta*. Let's see," he said and my mother instantly behaved like my sister. She secretly blinked an eye to me as if she was telling; "Only you and I are real players and your Dad is just a guest of few days, waiting for his flight to eternity."

I had already taken leave from department.

Ravin had booked a table at a well known "Icy Spicy" restaurant for our meeting.

Even though there was no possibility of Sid's interference, I suggested Ravin to fix our lunch time around 12.30 noon. Because at that time, Sid would be in the class.

We three and Ravin reached almost on the same time. He had worn orange *kurta* and blue jeans. Rado wrist watch. A thin sober gold chain on neck. It was peeping out from first button of his *kurta*. But, it was a saffron *tilak* on his forehead, which was making him look like the groom of any daily soap *saas-bahu* serial. Overall, he presented himself as a rich and desirable husband material. He shook hand with my Dad and touched feet of my mother.

We ordered from pure *veg* menu. In a decent language, Ravin kept informing the same details which I had told my parents in morning. They both also pretended as if they were listening to it for the first time. My mother pushed her limits of overacting.

Every mother of India knows the places where overacting is natural acting.

I kept observing nodding of my Dad. Ravin hardly provided any opportunity to them to ask anything. Every food item ordered was on the table and in an easy reach of all. Even though we all were helping each other by transferring spoons, salt, black pepper powder etc.

Everything was going perfectly. Ravin had done enough homework to keep conversations on. Though, there was no need, he started making a story from a real story happened recently.

"Uncle," he said. "Can you recognize something different on Shama's face?"

I surprised. I hadn't told him to reveal anything about it. They all started to study my face with much attention. Honestly, I didn't like it. Without waiting for any answers, Sid said, "Before a week, during their practical exam, fire blast incident happened to Shama. Her lab partner is a stupid boy who did mistake. Shama's workplace is too near to him. Her face was exposed to fire."

My mother stretched her eye muscles to observe my face. Now, even the waiter started to study my face. He was trying to find space between our conversation to ask if anymore we want to order or not.

"Shama," my Dad said. "You hadn't informed us all that."

I hated both gents over the lunch table, my investigative Dad and overreacting boyfriend. I told myself, "Why? Why they think so much unnecessarily?"

"I thought you would be disturbed without reason. So…" I said to my Dad.

"Why without reason? There is a reason to worry about. Isn't it? Whatever . . . then, what happened?" said my dad.

I imagined a detective kind of hat on his white haired head.

"I immediately took fire extinguisher and controlled the fire first," said Ravin. "Because the whole laboratory could catch fire because of it. Her nose skin was affected badly. I drove her to university health centre on my bike. You may see it healed so fast and wonderfully that if I haven't told you, you may never know. You can notice there is fresh glowing skin on her nose. It has slightly different hue than cheeks skin. Can you see the difference?"

I wondered that this man couldn't notice my swollen eyes, and now he is explaining so deep study of my face details.

By then, perhaps the waiter was satisfied by staring at me. He walked away.

"Now, if the story of bravery is over, may I say something?" Sid appeared from behind that waiter and said, "This brave hero had written to our HOD to relook on the matter of Shama's detention. So, Padmini Madam has sent me to inform you that dispute management committee of department want to see you both today. At 3 pm. So, be there on time. Bye."

"O… hello…boy, what is your name?" My Dad stopped him and said, "If this man is making a story, you tell the truth."

"Ravin," Sid said, "If incident happened by me on my working hood, why I am not affected at all? Uncle, why didn't you ask this brave man?"

I didn't react anything. Yet, I couldn't understand his intentions. Also, I wondered why my mother didn't interfere at all. She kept focusing on lunch without any hesitation. Even she kept ordering complimentary things like *kanda* and *chutney*. I wanted to ask Ravin why he didn't inform me if he had done any such complaint in written to HOD.

"Come come, Join us and tell the truth," my Dad said and invited Sid. A strange kind of smile was playing on my Dad's moustache.

Ravin wanted to say something but my mother pressed his hand under the table and stopped him to react anything.

Sid ordered orange juice and narrated the original incident. But, before my dad would say anything, my mother looked at Sid and said, "But, this is not *swayamvar* of my daughter and we are not in search of any suitable boy for her. I can see your orange juice is finished. So, you may leave now."

"I know it. I haven't presented myself as a candidate. I am here just on the order of Padmini Madam," said Sid.

By then, my detective Dad found out one more dimension of Sid.

"What is this *tattoo* expressing?"

My dad showed a tattoo on the bicep of Sid. "X-Sangeeta, Y-Avni, Z-" was written there in cursive writing.

"Sangeeta is my Ex-girlfriend. After her, Avni came to become my Y," Sid said.

He added some water in his finished glass of orange juice. He shook it a little and started sucking it with a straw. He finished it too and said, "I hope Z will be final girlfriend. Otherwise I will have to start from A again."

No one joined him in his laugh.

"Why did X and Y leave you?" said my Dad.

"They hadn't left me. We converted to friends. But, yes. I am no more dating any of them," said Sid.

He had dragged whole attention to him. It seemed as if we had gathered there to explore about Sid's personal life only.

"Sir, actually up to my third meeting date with Sangi, everything was fine. But, when I asked her to have medical checkup before moving to sex, she sent me SMS to full stop," said Sid.

My pure vegetarian mother made a face as if any non-vegan item was served to her.

"And Avni… Ah Avni! She didn't like that I had kept meeting Sangi, even after I and Avni started dating each other. Tell me Sir, where was I wrong? Shouldn't one undergo medical checkup before sex? Should one leave a nice friend? Just because, she doesn't believe in one of my ideas. My motto is unchangeable. Break up or set up, but be in style. Right style! What say?"

I came out of my chair.

"Come here," I said to Sid. He took little time to follow my order.

"Look at my eyes," I said. He looked. I slapped him with my full muscle energy. It changed his face direction towards outgoing door. He pressed his palm on his cheek which now had my palm's impression.

But, what he did then?

He moved to my Dad and said with a smiling face, "Sir… that much of effort is needed to make this girl doing something by her own hand."

16.

Before my dad would think to react anything, three policemen entered the restaurant as if they were just waiting outside to see some violence. One of them had an athletic body. Other two were following him with slow walk. They both liked cooling and appetizing smell of restaurant. Everyone watched them keeping their question of "why" silently on lips. I couldn't get why Sid looked so relaxed. Even though they hadn't asked anything yet, Sid said, "I think you want me. I am Siddharth. Let's go before this girl slaps me one more time."

"Did you make that sexy audio cassette?" Athletic policeman asked for reconfirmation.

Sid nodded proudly and started walking with them. He was telling me while going out, "Reach on time at department. Remember 3 pm. You too, brave boy."

I went with my parents to bus station to see off. Now they had just one hand bag.

"So, what I was telling, yes, keep yourself away from the boy like that, who has any relation with police station," my mother said and went inside the bus with her little hand bag.

My Dad came to me. He kept looking at me for little more time than usual. Perhaps he was trying to remember me with details. Somewhere in his mind, one thing was getting clear shape that he might be watching me for the last time- before the third and final heart attack.

"Shama, I am not against your choice. I really liked Ravin. No matter he just cooked up a bravery story. It happens. At his age, it happens. No harm in it. I had passed that age. He just wanted to keep conversation on. I am happy that he knew that silence, more than ten seconds in first meeting is not a good sign for concrete relations. Both parties must have real intentions to know about each other. He had looked at our dishes and predicted that we would take more two to three minutes more to finish it, so he told us a story. That's it. My main focus on this our final get-together is… are you going to make life or just going to rest under the shadow of someone's tree?"

Silence made its space between us. Then he went on, "In this dying time of mine, I realized that one should always give chance whoever keeps providing one "one more chance" back. So, try to choose the person who can give you "one more chance". Because, you see life hardly gives one more chance to anyone."

He put his hand upon his ill heart, on his chest.

My mother looked at us from the window of bus. She didn't find our 'little more talking' suitable for my future.

"The driver has arrived. Come inside now," she said. My dad followed it. Before leaving me, he hugged me for little more time than usual.

"Ok *beta*! Bye. Your Mamma doesn't want me to talk with you more. But, I have to convey what I want to. See something fell from your bag," he said.

There was a folded piece of paper around his legs. I touched his legs and picked up that paper. I understood him. I nodded with teary eyes. And then he left.

After their bus disappeared, I opened that paper and started reading.

Shama, you are just watching me dying, day by day, more and more, but I am experiencing it, heartbeat by heartbeat. So, I have some words about death. For reference, let me first tell you about life. Life is a tricky thing. It's just a vacation. One has to return from where he came. And to enjoy the vacation, to visit one place to another, one should deserve it. I am sorry to say, you are not that one deserving. You are just finding a tree to rest for whole vacation. Don't confuse. I don't say you have chosen wrong tree, I am concerned about your intentions.

You may have noticed I am talking lesser than earlier. It will keep on decreasing. And then, one day, I hardly have words to tell you. Even if I had words, I won't have the heart to convey them. Long back, before you started your graduation, I remember last time I told you to make life. And after that I never advised you anything.

See, my experience says death is not ultimate. It's dying. "Ing" is the engine which keeps death going on, even after final see off. Don't you know death speaks louder than life? So, perhaps after my death, I will keep talking to you. Obviously more than being alive. No one will be there to stop me. Not even your kind mother. You will not be able to ignore me. At that time, my words may scare you. They will easily find space to enter in you. Nightmares are those holes from were dead people talks to living ones.

And last thing, as everyone knows, a dying man never lies. So, believe me, Beta. I don't want to keep talking with anyone after death. I want you to free me. Do you know I am postponing third heart attack. Don't doubt. It's possible. But for what? Just to see you making a life. Being the deserving one for enjoying this vacation called life. Am I asking too much? No. I don't think it's too much. It's too easy. You are my girl.

I folded the paper and put it in my bag. Somewhere in my mind or heart, a decision was taking a perfect shape to gift at least one happy moment to my dad.

I came out of the bus station. Ravin had been waiting for me there.

"I hadn't written any letter for the matter of your detention, Shama, he was lying," he said. Again he couldn't notice my teary eyes.

"Thank god," I said.

"And I am coming from department," he said. "Nothing happened. But why did they arrest him? Do you know anything about the cassette they were talking about?"

"No," I said.

He drove me to my hostel. I wanted to listen to that second cassette which he forcefully gifted me. I just wanted to know what is there in that cassette which caused his arrest.

I saw my roommate girl on her bad with our common Sony walkman. She had inserted a *Natraj* pencil inside one of the hole of cassette and trying to circling it.

"Our walkman's fast forward switch is not working," she said.

I just thought to tell her to give me the cassette and walkman. But before that she said, "Do you know I had intentionally passed ten days to enjoy this new cassette and new fantasy? I love to enjoy such audio fantasy after long break. By the way, who did give this cassette to you?"

"You please finish listening to it and give me as early as possible. I have passed eleven days," I said.

I regretted for forgetting to listen it even though I had it from so many days. I drown off in thinking of what would be there in that cassette.

After an hour, roommate girl came out of bathroom. She was done with it.

"I don't want to know how it was." I disappointed her by telling her such words.

I just took walkman, sat earphones comfortably, pushed the play button and cut myself from the world around. The familiar and confident voice of Sid started entering inside me.

17.

Thank you all for making my first audio story a grand success. A lot of people have written to me, of course without mentioning their identity. They asked questions about my life. It's not convenient to write back to each of them. So, I am telling you my little biography and thereby I'm going to answer most of your questions. After that, I promise you, I will tell my second audio story. But, if you are not interested in my life and want to listen to the main thing immediately, you can fast forward this cassette. Who am I to prevent your weapons from war? A war for sexiness with self!

So, let me start. It was an evening time of 1st June 1998, when I reached a beautiful, small, educational town named Vidyanagar by a state transport bus. There was a light drizzling rain. I came out of the bus station with my *Aristocrat* suitcase. I saw a small book shop which had plastic roof extended to save books from rain. I stood under there to save myself from rain. I waited for quite some time and some books dragged my attention. Books were shining due to the yellow light of a bulb. There were cheap roadside novels, *Vaibhav laxmi vrat* kind of religious booklets, filmy magazines like *Mayapuri* and some second hand books.

There was a picture of a crying child on the cover of one book. The child was surrounded by a cloud of dust. A man with a long gun was standing in front of the child. The gunman had raised one foot to kick on the shoulder of the child. The untold words of the complaining eyes of child had been written under the picture. "I am going to tell all this to God." My eyes didn't stop on the picture. I was not mature enough to understand the pain and hopelessness of that child.

But, my age was enough to understand adultery. My eyes stopped on the cover of book which had an adult picture. The naked woman pressed her hands on the back of a man as if she was pulling her closer. The woman's eyes were closed but the lines on her face were saying that you can be the man who is in between her hands. Title of book was written in bold and black letters. "*Bhigi bhigi kahaniya*- Only eleven rupees." There was no mention of author's name. I was driven by my curiosity and bought it. I didn't have one rupee change. But, shopkeeper said, "It's ok." His experience had probably told him that one rupee should be left for a possible regular customer. He hanged another similar book there. He had been trying to show me that he had a collection of such books.

At that time, I didn't realize that the purchase of that ten rupees book will not stay as a private thing but will result in a secret popularity. I admitted to the hostel of my caste. Very soon, I had a group of friends having similar habits. Sorry, similar dirty habits!

In the hostel, the book was secretly circulated from one hand to another, from one room to another. The book had something which was making it a reread quality book. Whoever read it, he had to come back to my door again in around four days.

One day, three boys came together to me for the book. All of them were in such a mental stage that no one of them was ready to postpone the thing; they used to do after reading that book.

After some arguments, I said, "Let me read it and you all listen together."

All agreed instantly or perhaps they had no time to think of any other ways. They closed door and windows of my room. I started reading the story. After first page, I started to pay attention to all the necessary ups and downs in delivery of narration. The imagination of the story was spreading slowly on the faces of all three.

We four weren't looking at each other. Actually that was the maximum privacy we could manage there. They were connected with my voice. Sometimes they pinched the zip of their pant and pull it upwards to provide oxygen inside the underwear. Although they three knew the erotic story, they wanted to let it thrill themselves. They liked to hear the details again about how everything happened.

It is the biggest magic of the story that we knowingly let it to cheat ourselves again and again.

They three left happily. They couldn't stop themselves from telling others about the new way I found out. I had discovered my inner narrator.

After a week, they came back to me with other seven boys. The strength kept increasing gradually. They started to come with new such books available at the book shop outside the bus station. But, there were only four books they got. The time came when I had an audience of twenty two boys in front of me. All knew the stories but they were addicted to my voice and style of narration. I thought they may feel boring to hear the same stories again and again. I experimented to mix the stories by connecting them differently. But, most of them opposed me almost immediately. Perhaps everyone's fantasy had taken a solid shape inside them. They were not ready to change a single word. So, I had to keep telling same stories. I also never wanted to loss my loving audience. Very soon I became much fluent and I hardly had to read from the book. Every sentence I remembered by heart. I felt as if I was a religious guru, *pandit* or *kathakar* sat on a big and heightened chair. They all sat with silence and seriousness in front of me as if we would have been gathered for prayer or *bhajan sandhya* or something like that. A unique style of narration had been developed in me effortlessly.

Whole first year of college had been passed like that. Most of us had been failed and some had ATKT in two subjects. Those who had ATKT were feeling as if they got gold medal. I was among the failed ones. Because religious guru, *pandit* or *kathakar* had to go to the hell first. And then followers would join them there.

My father said exactly what I expected.

"Sid, now if you want to continue your study, you have to manage money yourself."

My father had a unique habit. He never said no for anything. He always gave chance but also charge for earning it. I loved him for this unique quality. He had very less expectations from me after I scored just 44% in 12th science. Also my brother was helping and learning our family business too well. My younger sister was decent looking. She was an average girl in study. But better than me. At least she never failed.

One day, when I called my mother and requested her to help me for some money, she said, "Your father thinks that you can't manage money and will join our business in some days. I also think so, Sid."

Actually, I was already agreed with my parents" prediction. But, before that, I wanted to give me one more chance. I had decided to not go home for at least one year.

How shameless I was? I was missing my time as a religious guru, *pandit* or *kathakar*. At least I had something to do. I hated those past classmates who had ATKT and were going to college. So, when one of them dared to ask me whether I could read stories for them again, I said, "No. Never ask me again or I will chop your penis and then tell story." He took time to register my warning in his mind. Yes, same as you, my dear listeners.

I heard a gossip about me. One boy, who had new red pimples, was telling to another, "*Yaar*, everyone knows the stories but only Sid's narration has that magic we are addicted to. Can you believe? I haven't seen inside my underwear from last two weeks. Can you believe? Two weeks of this sexy monsoon."

Another boy replied, "And that is why pimples are started appearing on your face. I read in a newspaper column that if we don't let that *Dove* shampoo kind of liquid out of our underwear, it tries to come out as pimples."

I never responded anything to gossips. But when I found a lonely time in my room, I stood against the mirror. I observed my cheeks had color and lines of pride. I had a proud for the fact that I was still in demand. My heart loved that lightly disgusting reputation. Not just because of my demand as a storyteller in boys, but also due to one more reason. That confidence of storytelling in front more than twenty boys had melted my old rigid complex of stage fear.

At the age of nine, when I was in fourth standard, I participated in the school oratory competition. I reached the centre of stage with slow steps and adjusted my hairs before starting my speech. I kept murmuring of the first sentence of my speech from around last five minutes. A peon came to me and he arranged mike with my height. When he was done, I saw my friend in the first raw of audience. He was trying to hint me something I couldn't understand. But, I got him when he practically showed me. He was doing up and down of his zip of pant continuously. He was so close friend of mine that I understood his silent lisping too. He was clearly telling, "Stupid, your zip is open."

It disturbed me so much that I forgot the very first sentence of my speech. I kept speaking anything from anywhere in my memory of speech draft. The only meaning of my entire stage time of nearly one minute was that I should leave the stage as soon as possible. After that incident, I couldn't gather the confidence to step on any ladder of any stage for years.

When one fails for the first time on a stage event in childhood, it leaves a scar so deep it stays as a stage fear for a lifetime.

The boy, who had red pimples, came to me when I was having last sip of my last tea. With that sip, all my money was finished. I was well aware of that. I looked at him. His face hardly had one square inch clear skin without pimple.

"*Yaar* Sid," he said. "Thirty four into fifty is seventeen hundred rupees. You can earn if you wish."

"How?" I asked.

Thirty four boys, including me, want to hear live story from you; fifty rupees per session. One session will be of thirty five minutes approximately, like we had last year. Tell me if you are interested. By the way, I had taken all money in advance. This is it. You can keep if you are going to do it tonight."

He gave me the money. I took it and ordered another tea, which was famous as the golden tea, my favorite.

I kept doing such storytelling sessions frequently. Sometimes, two times a week. I earned money which was enough for my study and living simply. I never forgot that it was a last chance and it must not be missed. I couldn't imagine myself being happy at our family business. I could pass all three subjects and saved myself. My parents were surprised and asked me about how I survived. I had to make a believable and acceptable story. And it was not difficult thing for me.

Those, who were much fond of my live storytelling, gifted me a Sony walkman on my birthday. I saw a red button which was labeled as "record". I tried recording something like one, two, four, one, two, four. An idea came to my mind that I should record my stories and sell the cassettes wherever I can manage. I recorded the story. I ordered to make fifty copies at music shop. But, I had no idea for selling it. An old music shop owner told me that he would help me. He knew from his long experience about how mouth publicity works in music industry. I had no reason to disagree. He started giving my one cassette free with each walkman sold. He had contacts in three nearby cities. In around a month, he told me that we had an order of total two hundred thirty copies of cassette from other cities. It earned me more money than live story narration. In next three months, I had a producer who wanted me to prepare one more cassette with better sound quality. And the result, you are hearing me now on that cassette.

Now, before starting new audio story, one last thing I want to say to all of you. In our country, there is no source of sex education. Except those three pages in science textbook of ninth standard. We are on our own totally. Isn't it?

These stories help us to know whatever is needed to know about sex. This interesting way provides us an imagination to get relief from sexual tension. Haven't you experienced that after discharge, a satisfactory discharge, how fresh we feel?

After every satisfactory discharge, I always had a feeling to do well in life, in study. That is very important moment to capture. On that particular moment, one should kick start whatever one wants to do.

From personal experience, I can say that it is better to listen to such stories and have good discharge. It takes only forty five minutes total. Isn't it a good deal than wasting weeks to run behind girls? And for girls to crave for boys? We all have capacity and dreams of travelling to Mars. But our country has forced us to circle around each other's waist? So, this time, don't miss that moment.

It is my second intention of making this cassette.

First one is money. No doubt in it.

Now, let me start the main erotica, especially for which you are listening to me. Please fasten your zips. And girls, fasten the hook of your pink bra. I am on the edge of pouring magic of "*aabra ka dabra*, hooks and zips are going to *khul ja simsim*."

* * *

I'm twenty four and I'm 5.9 ft tall. Average built.

I was doing my graduation in Bangalore, staying alone in a rented room.

It all started when I had a huge crush on my rich neighbor's girl who was entering her 30's at that time. She was around 5.6 ft with bra size 32D. Her body was milky white and silky smooth. She had long legs and pear-shaped back and I used to think about her amazing body every day.

I used to gaze her every time when she was doing string jump exercises in the second floor gallery of her duplex. Her cleavage was heaving and shrinking as if it was inviting me. I think she understood as she caught me staring at her several times.

She used to spend more time in her gallery.

Since her parents had gone to visit a relative, she was alone that day. From the gallery, she showed me two movie tickets and pointed a finger towards her car, parked on the service lane. I understood immediately and agreed happily. I had showed her thumbs up in agreement. She noticed the grin on my face and came to know why I was happy. She was also kind of excited. I got ready in five minutes. And we set off in her car. She was driving and suggested that we go for a movie and will be back before her parents come back.

"So... when will they come back?" I asked.

"Tomorrow," she said, without looking at me.

It was a romantic movie. We bought popcorn and took a rear seat.

Before I describe the story, let me describe what she was wearing. It was a red & black body fit kurti and tight black leggings. She was wearing a pink panty. I got to that because when she got into the car, her top was stuck to the door and raised it all the way to the top and I saw her pink panty which was worn slightly above the leggings.

She noticed me staring at that and gave a naughty smile and said, "At least keep your mouth closed while staring at girls."

For which I fake laughed, fairly embarrassed.

The movie then started. I'm sure that she had intentionally chosen that movie to watch. After few minutes, all the kissing scenes started and I was turned on a little bit. And so was she, because I could see her erected nipples leave a mark on her top which was clearly visible when there was a bright scene on the screen.

Since there was only one popcorn bucket which I was holding, she had to reach and grab every time she wanted it. I held the popcorn paper bowl on my bulge. It was a turn on trick. A moment came when I moved the bowl to my left hand and her hand directly came and grabbed my bulge. Oh boy! That was a wonderful feeling. It was like an electric shock through the veins of my dick.

Since she was embarrassed, she asked sorry but I could see that she was more turned on since she could feel my dick through my jeans. There were many erotic scenes in the movie which just added more fuel to our fire.

The movie ended and we were walking back to the car. She took up the topic of the incident which took place.

She said, "Sorry for the incident."

"That's ok. It was by accident."

"By the way, why was your dick hard? Were you turned on by the movie scenes?"

I was stunned because I was not expecting her to ask such question.

"Yeah, I guess even you were?" I said hesitatingly, without looking at her.

"Don't be shy. I can admit even I was turned on."

I took the green signal and started being comfortable.

She then asked me if I do those things with my girlfriend. I told her that I am a virgin and I don't have a girlfriend to have that experience, for which she grinned and said, "Poor you."

Then I asked her, "You might be having those experiences all the time."

With a frowning face she replied, "No. Not really. We are same. I'm as poor as you are in this matter."

Since she was sad, I offered her a hug to make her feel better. The hug was amazing. She pressed her entire body on me and I was fully turned on when I felt her pointy nipples and soft boobs on my chest. Oh, that was amazing and I was rock hard. Her soft hot body pressed against my bulge and I was shivering with joy. She could feel the bulge and didn't hesitate and pressed even more.

Then we decided to drive back home. We both were aroused because of the hug. It was a complete silence in the car on the way back.

In the middle of the journey, she asked me if I enjoyed the movie. I replied saying, "What's not to enjoy in that?" with a slight wink.

She gave a naughty smile and asked if I watch such movies.

Then I replied, "Yeah, romantic movies? Others also sometimes. A young guy needs to be updated with those," which made her laugh.

Then all of a sudden, she asked me, "Do you have feelings for me?" I was a little shocked and I asked, "What do you mean?"

"I have seen you giving me that kind of look."

"Yeah a little bit. I find you extremely beautiful and... "

"And... what?"

"Hot!"

She smiled at me and stopped her car after a while near an alley.

"You want to experience the things which we saw in the movie today?"

With joy and confusion, I replied, "With you? Isn't that inappropriate?"

"Yeah, with me. And no need to think about its appropriateness. It's our personal thing. Moreover, we have feelings for each other."

Before I could start my sentence she grabbed me and planted a kiss on my lips.

Her soft pink lips felt frantically thirsty. She sucked on my upper lip while I was sucking her lower one. After a while, she started playing with my tongue using hers. God! That felt amazing. It was as if her soft tongue was about to melt in my mouth. She tasted good so even I started sucking her mouth. This went on for fifteen minutes and she started rubbing my thighs and proceeded towards my zip. She started rubbing my already hard dick above my pants. And it was almost visible since it left a print on the pant.

I saw this as a green signal and started rubbing her hips. I worked my way towards her pear shaped ass. Wow, it was the perfect shape and size! I started pressing it above her clothes.

I am grateful to the person who invented leggings. It was like I was touching her bare ass.

I then slowly inserted my hand inside her leggings. I could feel her thin panty and all I could think of was tearing it off using my teeth.

I could see in her face that she was very excited to see my cock. She stared at it.

She hesitates for a moment, then lowers my boxers, pulls out my rock-hard cock, and cradles it gently in her hand. Like she's making sure of something, the way a doctor takes a pulse. With her soft hand touching me, I felt a stray thought, maybe-spring up in my crotch.

She put my dick in her wet mouth filled with her juicy saliva. She rolled her tongue over the top of my dick putting my entire 6 inch in her mouth and was squeezing my balls.

Hell yeah! It felt great. I felt like I would become unconscious because I was shivering with pleasure.

She looked at my eyes and said, "It's yummy."

I grinned at her and continued enjoying the sweet pleasure of her warm mouth on my erect dick. I moved my hands into her top, feeling her buttery and juicy boobs over her purple bra. I squeezed the left boob and she moaned.

All while she was sucking me.

I moved my hand behind her top and tried to unhook her bra. I was unsuccessful and she looked at me and said, "See this is what I'm here to teach you."

Then she guided my fingers onto her bra hook and unhooked the bra and said, "See this is how you do it. Learn it properly because you have to do it often for me," and winked and continued sucking my cock which was covered by her sweet saliva and my pre-cum.

I slowly removed her bra and grabbed one of her free hot organ. Damn, it was just the right shape and size! It felt warm and soft that all I could think of is filling my mouth with that beautiful breast of hers. I could feel her erected nipple and I played with it by drawing gentle circle around it with my fingers. It felt so good.

Since she was blowing my cock from the driver's seat, I didn't have access to her pussy so I used my hands on her boobs. I was rubbing it well and I knew that she was enjoying it because I could hear her sweet moans. She kept moaning every time she took out my dick from her mouth. It turned me on more.

This continued for around few minutes and finally, I was about to come. I asked her if she is comfortable taking my cum in her mouth, for which she nodded. I grabbed her silky hair and started moving my hips up and down with my dick in her mouth.

After few seconds I came in her mouth and she licked my dick clean and said, "We don't want to waste it. Do we?"

I was over excited. It was all like a wet dream. The girl who I used to dream about just sucked my dick and licked my cum.

I just wanted to see her naked and have a hot steamy night right then.

After a while, she started the car again and told me, "Let's go home now. We have the whole night ahead and I don't want anyone to catch us doing it over here."

By then, it was raining. She closed the windows of car. We finally reached her home. After she closed the main door of her drawing room, we rushed in her room near the gallery. My heart was pounding. Outside, it was raining heavily.

We threw ourselves on her spring bed. We removed each others' clothes. There was no mark on her shining skin except a mole on her shoulder. Her nipples were looking like two brown kishmish on her silvery skin of breasts.

She had cum as I could see her cream flowing out. I went down kissing her stomach navel and her cunt which was thick and wet. She had cleanly shaved pink pussy. I felt it seductive and no doubt it tasted well too.

I now started to lick her pussy lips, with my hands spreading her legs. She moaned loud as I inserted my tongue into her pussy, which her moaning sounds as the background score, she was holding my head tight and pushed it more towards her pussy. I sucked her cunt for about ten minutes by now my dick was hard again for the final kill. I felt as if my heart would have pumped all my blood towards my dick.

Her juice was all over my lips and tongue. I licked her well just like a dog and I knew she was enjoying it, and so was I. She pulled me up and she asked me to fuck her. I crept over her body and she held my dick and guided it to her tight, lusty hole.

The minute I pushed it in, she moaned out loud and hugged me tight. Her legs were locked behind my back. While she was pressing me towards her, her long girly nails scratched my back a bit. I also moaned once, like her. I slowly started rubbing my hard dick in and out of her pussy hole. Her pussy was wet enough to slide my cock freely. They were supporting each other so well as if they were made for each other. There was a pleasant friction between her pussy skin with my dick. She sucked my lip when I pushed my dick a bit harder. She was glowing with every single stroke I gave her. That spring bed also started moaning with her. I was on cloud nine. My desires had come true. I fucked her as hard as I could do. Finally, we climaxed again together. She took every single drop of my juice in her hot pussy.

We smooched again for few moments and then moved in for a shower.

* * *

Siddharth was quite right. Quality of this cassette was much better than his first cassette titled "LISTEN ONLY, WHEN YOU ARE LONELY (1)" Real sounds of moaning, some male-female foreplay conversation and sound of rain were creating over-sensual effect. Very soon Sid's voice reached to the triangle located between my legs. It demanded support of my hand. I surrendered to it happily. There was no guilt feeling this time. I had believed his words which were telling that it's perfectly fine to release sexual tension. This cassette gave me what was expected, actually more than that.

After washing myself, I thought of Sid as a man who entered inside hundreds of under wears by such stories.

Yet, there was some reel of cassette remaining to be heard. I started listening to it too.

Now Sid's tone had changed. It sounded as if it was coming from too far like from some other world. From skyline...

He was telling . . .

I have heard that there was once an ancient and majestic tree, with branches spreading out towards the sky. When it was in a flowering mood, butterflies of all shapes, colors and sizes danced around it. When it grew blossoms and bore fruit, birds from far lands came and sang in it. The branches, like outstretched hands, blessed all who came and sat in their shade. A small boy used to come and play under it, and the big tree developed affection for the small boy.

Love between big and small is possible, if the big is not aware that it is big. The tree didn't know it was big; only man has that kind of knowledge. The big always has the ego as its prime concern, but for love, nobody is big or small. Love embraces whoever comes near.

So the tree developed a love for this small boy who used to come to play near it. Its branches were high, but it bent and bowed them down so that he might pluck its flowers and pick its fruit. Love is ever ready to bow; the ego is never ready to bend. If you approach the ego, its branches will stretch upwards even more; it will stiffen so you cannot reach it.

The playful child came, and the tree bowed its branches. The tree was very pleased when the child plucked some flowers; its entire being was filled with the joy of love. Love is always happy when it can give something; the ego is always happy when it can take.

The boy grew. Sometimes he slept on the tree's lap, sometimes he ate its fruit, and sometimes he wore a crown of the tree's flowers and acted like a jungle king. One becomes like a king when the flowers of love are there, but one becomes poor and miserable when the thorns of the ego are present. To see the boy wearing a crown of flowers and dancing about filled the tree with joy, it nodded in love; it sang in the breeze. The boy grew even more. He began to climb the tree to swing on its branches. The tree felt very happy when the boy rested on its branches. Love is happy when it gives comfort to someone; the ego is only happy when it gives discomfort.

With the passage of time the burden of other duties came to the boy. Ambition grew; he had exams to pass; he had friends to chat with and to wander about with, so he did not come often. But the tree waited anxiously for him to come. It called from its soul, "Come. Come. I am waiting for you." Love waits day and night. And the tree waited. The tree felt sad when the boy did not come. Love is sad when it can't share; love is sad when it can't give. Love is grateful when it can share. When it can surrender, totally, love is the happiest.

As he grew, the boy came less and less to the tree. The man who becomes big, whose ambitions grow, finds less and less time for love. The boy was now engrossed in worldly affairs.

One day, while he was passing by, the tree said to him, "I wait for you but you do not come. I expect you daily."

The boy said, "What do you have? Why should I come to you? Have you any money? I am looking for money." The ego is always motivated. Only if there is some purpose to be served will the ego come. But love is motiveless. Love is its own reward.

The startled tree said, "You will come only if I give something?" That which withholds is not love. The ego amasses, but love gives unconditionally. "We don't have that sickness, and we are joyful," the tree said. "Flowers bloom on us. Many fruits grow on us. We give soothing shade. We dance in the breeze, and sing songs. Innocent birds hop on our branches and chirp even though we don't have any money. The day we get involved with money, we will have to go to the temples like you weak men do, to learn how to obtain peace, to learn how to find love. No, we do not have any need for money."

The boy said, "Then why should I come to you? I will go where there is money. I need money." The ego asks for money because it needs power. The tree thought for a while and said, "Don't go anywhere else, my dear. Pick my fruit and sell it. You will get money that way."

The boy brightened immediately. He climbed up and picked all fruit of the tree; even the unripe ones were shaken down. The tree felt happy, even though some twigs and branches were broken, even though some of its leaves had fallen to the ground. Getting broken also makes love happy, but even after getting, the ego is not happy. The ego always desires more. The tree didn't notice that the boy hadn't even once looked back to thank him. It had had its thanks when the boy accepted the offer to pick and sell its fruit.

The boy did not come back for a long time. Now he had money and he was busy making more money from that money. He had forgotten all about the tree. Years passed. The tree was sad. It yearned for the boy's return - like a mother whose breasts are filled with milk but whose son is lost. Her whole being craves for her son; she searches madly for her son so he can come to lighten her. Such was the inner cry of that tree. Its entire being was in agony.

After many years, now an adult, the boy came to the tree.

The tree said, "Come, my boy. Come embrace me."

The man said, "Stop that sentimentality. That was a childhood thing. I am not a child anymore." The ego sees love as madness, as a childish fantasy.

But the tree invited him: "Come, swing on my branches. Come dance. Come play with me."

The man said, "Stop all this useless talk! I need to build a house. Can you give me a house?"

The tree exclaimed: "A house! I am without a house." Only men live in houses. Nobody else lives in a house but man. And do you notice his condition after his confinement among four walls? The bigger his buildings, the smaller man becomes. "We do not stay in houses, but you can cut and take away my branches - and then you may be able to build a house."

Without wasting any time, the man brought an axe and severed all the branches of the tree. Now the tree was just a bare trunk. But love cares not for such things — even if its limbs are severed for the loved one. Love is giving; love is ever ready to give.

The man didn't even bother to thank the tree. He built his house. And the days flew into years.

The trunk waited and waited. It wanted to call for him, but it had neither branches nor leaves to give it strength. The wind blew by, but it couldn't even manage to give the wind a message. And still its soul resounded with one prayer only: "Come. Come, my dear. Come." But nothing happened.

Time passed and the man had now become old. Once he was passing by and he came and stood by the tree.

The tree asked, "What else can I do for you? You have come after a very, very long time."

The old man said, "What else can you do for me? I want to go to distant lands to earn more money. I need a boat, to travel."

Cheerfully, the tree said, "But that's no problem, my love. Cut my trunk, and make a boat from it. I would be so very happy if I could help you go to faraway lands to earn money. But, please remember, I will always be awaiting your return."

The man brought a saw, cut down the trunk, made a boat and sailed away.

Now the tree is a small stump. And it waits for its loved one to return. It waits and it waits and it waits. The man will never return; the ego only goes where there is something to gain and now the tree has nothing, absolutely nothing to offer. The ego does not go where there is nothing to gain. The ego is an eternal beggar, in a continuous state of demand, and love is charity. Love is a king, an emperor! Is there any greater king than love?

I was resting near that stump one night. It whispered to me, "That friend of mine has not come back yet. I am very worried in case he might have drowned, or in case he might be lost. He may be lost in one of those faraway countries. He might not even be alive any more. How I wish for news of him! As I near the end of my life, I would be satisfied with some news of him at least. Then I could die happily. But he would not come even if I could call him. I have nothing left to give and he only understands the language of taking."

18.

I took out earphones. I realized I was crying. But, when I touched corners of my eyes, I couldn't find any wetness. I suddenly felt thirsty. I thought there must be enough water inside me from which tears can be formed. I drank some water and sprinkled over my face. I wanted relief from my over thinking about the pain of lover tree. I decided to leave my room immediately to go out. Anywhere. Just anywhere.

I wrapped a shawl and got out of my hostel. I started walking opposite to the way of department. I saw some people, cutting a big *Gulmahor* tree on the side of way. I stopped but couldn't say anything. Tears were now formed from the water I drank. They came out themselves. I moved on from there and stopped an auto-rickshaw.

"Police station," I said. Driver looked at my teary eyes and said, "What happened? May I suggest you something before you involve police in any of your matter?"

"No. Just drive me there."

During the ride, he kept throwing glances at me by mirror in front of driving seat.

"Please focus on the road and not me," I said in low and firm voice. After that I don't know whether he looked in that mirror or not.

I ignored him and looked outside the rickshaw. There were hurrying clouds in the sky with a false brightness which had no warmth in it, and the wind was penetrating through my shawl and traditional dress. It was colder than every January.

When we reached police station, driver advised me, "Only money and contacts works at this place. I hope you have at least anyone of them."

I had none of them. Even I reached there without my purse. I had no money to pay to driver. I found it too difficult to find words. I realized I had made a mistake by behaving strangely.

"*Bhaiya*, I forgot my purse at hostel. Now . . ." I said.

"Oh… then, how will you manage in this police station?" he said.

"No no. That is not too important. But I don't have money to pay you too."

He gave me three thousand rupees. And said, "Keep it. That's all I have in my pocket. Back me tomorrow morning at 9. I will be at the gate of the girl's hostel. Don't worry."

I kept that money with hesitation.

"Sorry, I shouldn't behave like that. You are too kind," I said, looking down.

"See you tomorrow," he said and left with smile. I stood with gratitude.

It was the second time I had been at the police station. First time, I visited it for my passport enquiry. Procedures had been completed in five minutes, in just two hundred rupees. I didn't ask for the receipt and they hadn't given. My mother had told me, "Get a passport. NRI boys come for too short time in India to get married. If someone is in your fate, you must have at least passport ready with you."

I entered inside the big gate named in red letters. "Vidyanagar Police Station"

"Yes, tell me," a constable came to me and said in polite and respectful voice. I recognized him. I had seen him when they arrested Sid from that restaurant.

"I want to meet inspector Sir," I said.

"What's the use? He will send you to me only."

"I want to see a boy-you arrested yesterday from Icy Spicy restaurant," I said in requesting voice.

"What is your relation with him?"

"I am his younger sister," I said. I thought to play safely.

"Why you three sisters don't talk to each other?"

"What do you mean?" I said.

"Two girls already came here to visit him. They both introduced themselves as his younger sisters."

Before I tried to fabricate any more detail, he said, "Give five hundred rupees, no one will ask you anything and you can meet him."

He said as if he was explaining a standard official procedure. I paid it. I followed him to reach the inspector.

"Sir, third sister," Constable showed thumbs up sign. Inspector did the same. Inspector told me to take a seat in front of him. After a time, voices murmured and I heard Siddharth's laugh. He was in the same unwashed clothes.

"Shama!" he said.

Before I quite knew what he was about, he had bent and kissed my cheek, his three days old mustache hair tickling me. I felt something comforting and exciting about his grip on my cold back side. I said to myself, "Whatever he says in his audio story, jail couldn't change that attitude in him."

"Follow me towards the meeting room," Constable said.

"Sir," I moved to inspector and said, "I had listened to his cassette. If you would have listened, you could not arrest Siddharth. Don't believe me. But please listen it once."

"We have arrested him for this cassette. Have you had this one?" he said, showing me the cassette which had a label, "LISTEN ONLY, WHEN YOU ARE LONELY (1)"

I had nothing to say now. He was arrested for part 1. I was advocating him for part two.

"Part two is not yet so popular that it can cause arrest," said Inspector.

"Sir," Sid interfered, "May I talk to my sister in person for a minute?"

He allowed us and constable took us to a small meeting room. Then he left us alone.

"Oh Shama," Siddharth said. "I couldn't believe when constable told me that you have come here."

"First you tell me why did you take advantage of my

helplessness? How dare you to hug me?" I said. But there were no lines of anger on my face. My sentence seemed too artificial, even to me.

"I am a father of *Gandhiji*. If someone slaps me, I kiss back on cheek. Just one condition, that one must be a girl. Now please, don't complain about my unshaved face. There is no facility to shave here."

"You perfectly understand what I am trying to say," I said.

"Actually we can kiss here more intensely. We are so alone. Isn't it?" he said while his eyes sought my lips and lingered there a moment.

"Try it to have one more slap," I said.

"Then, leave this talk of carnal desires," Sid said. "You always drag me in that. Tell me why do you want me to get free from here? How rogue I was? I didn't take your side when you did that blast in the lab."

"Don't ask me anything. And please, don't predict about my thoughts. I don't think you deserve to be here. That's it. No more. No less. I don't know how to help you. You tell me how can I? I just have twenty five hundred rupees in my pocket."

"Well, in that case, I can come out myself. Let's go," he said.

I could trust him without asking how. I saw a kind of confidence on his face. I followed him.

We sat around the table of inspector.

"Sir," Sid said, "May I talk to you secretly for a while?"

"Why? Tell me here," said Inspector.

He looked at me and then at inspector, "She is really my sister. I should not discuss that thing in front of her."

They both moved to a window in a corner. Siddharth told me later about what they talked.

"There is a financer-producer behind this cassette project. Only by his help of money, we managed to get so much popularity and sell," he had told him.

"Really? Who?" he asked.

"I think it's dangerous to speak his name. Let me write it."

He wrote a name of a district collector and his contact number on the wooden window.

"This is direct and personal number of him. Not of PA or any one. Call this number and say "Siddharth," he will praise about my second cassette and give you figures of sales of it. You can check it right now. Let's call from any STD PCO."

And then, we were out of police station in next two minutes. I was more relieved than happy. He was normal as if he would be frequent visitor of police station.

One girl ran towards us from the entry gate of compound of police station. She looked like villager. She was more traditionally dressed than me. I had seen such girls in paintings. Her look reminded me of *Rajashthani* women who used to wear lots of green bangles and other ornaments. But she had sharp features which were difficult to hide from the sight of beauty observer like me. She hugged Sid with the momentum of her run. That constable was walking around there. "Sister number one," he commented. Siddharth hadn't heard him or ignored knowingly.

"Sangi, why do you come again, *yaar*?" Sid scolded her lightly. Her name reminded me his *tattoo*, "X-Sangeeta, Y-Avni, Z-"

"I thought I would manage to provide you my home made food," she said.

"Oh girls, if you all will love me so much, I will stay in jail forever," Sid said.

Though, there was no reason, I didn't like her. I think I wouldn't hate her if she wouldn't hug him too tight and bring that *tiffin*.

"If you love me so much, then why do you never let me kiss even once?" Siddharth said, looking at Sangeeta.

"First go and have medical tests of your saliva and lip's skin, then I will think, Mr. Over thinker," she replied.

I knew why she said like that. At restaurant, Siddharth had already explained the reason of his break up with her. He had demanded medical checkup before sex. She had refused to do it.

"Oh god, you girls always drag me to the talk of sexual desires," Sid continued in his teasing mood.

He introduced me and Sangeeta.

"Shama, meet Sangeeta. In my second cassette, the voice of moaning is hers."

I hated her more after knowing that she had contributed in that cassette too.

"Ok. I am Shama," I said but we didn't shake hand.

"Let's eat this food together somewhere," Siddharth suggested.

"No no," Sangeeta said hurriedly. "I am going. I just came to see you and give you *tiffin*. I am so happy seeing you relieved and fine." And then she left.

During coming back to my hostel in the auto rickshaw, I asked him about Avni. Yes. About that girl's name on his tattoo "Y-Avni".

"She came yesterday to see me," Sid said. "But as she saw me with Sangi, she left without saying a word. She is a little that kind of girl. But she is really a… "

"That's it," I said, cutting his sentence. "Don't narrate her biography and your history of make outs with her."

"Ok. Later. In leisure time," he said. "See, we reached your hostel now."

He waved a hand to greet his gatekeeper friend. And then we separated.

19.

I wondered how I forgot to ask Sid why he had lied that Ravin had complained to the HOD about my detention. I kept thinking of possible reasons and got bored shortly. I looked at my walkman and the cassette on my study table. It reminded me the image of dying tree. Over-thinking easily finds a sad image among the stock inside the mind.

My problem was that I had options. What to choose? Helpless mother was insisting for Ravin. Dying Dad was telling to make a life.

I had no real trust on Sid. He could say anything in cassettes and do anything in life. Thinking of love with Sid was too far thing to even think. Even though I hated Sangeeta and Avni both, I had more hate for Sangeeta who brought tiffin for Sid at jail. Less hatred for Avni. I didn't have any idea how to hate a person without knowing her shape. I managed to imagine her shape and hated her a little.

I couldn't find any strong and proper reason to hate or love Ravin.

Everything became clear when I decided to be practical. My mother was the most happy for my decision. She started humming a Gujarati bridal farewell song for me in advance. She sung only when my Dad would not around because lyrics of the song also had a kind of feeling as if one is leaving his beloved world forever. I confirm that I took that quick decision in expectation of closing the windows of options. I wanted to focus on "making a life" to see my Dad dying happily. In short, I was fixing my long term future with Ravin. And by closing other options, I wanted to just focus on study and make a life.

I had taken three days of leave from department. I reached my home town just after a day my parents reached. They didn't advise me to think again. Perhaps my Dad had noticed a kind of confidence in my eyes. I just told him, "Believe me, Dad, I am going to set you free. Very soon you will see me becoming deserving for vacation."

They had now enough reasons to be happy for my decision. My mother had been preparing for my engagement from long time. She called a girl from beauty parlor who designed *mahendi* on my hand. I applied a lemon juice on it and after few hours, when I saw my deep dark brown designed hands and red painted nails, I thought I was ready.

"If you would have taken enough time," my mother had said, "you could have long beautiful girly nails. But it's ok. It's just an engagement. For marriage, we will have enough time to manage everything."

"How will you manage the thing which is constantly nearing to Dad?" I said. "Can you postpone his death?" I disappointed her by saying that. After her five minutes silence and two big cold tears, I also regretted for my words.

Next morning, Ravin and his parents with few core family members travelled to my home town in their upper middle class cars. They had to park their cars in the common plot of our society. We didn't have a car or even space for a car parking. In the short ceremony, I was engaged to Ravin. We exchanged rings. Both families befooled each other knowingly. We both were appreciated for lot of qualities and talents which we never had.

When we found solitude, Ravin came nearer in that perfumed atmosphere of occasion. He smelled same as earlier when we were on the shore of a canal. It reminded me whatever happened at that time. I never liked artificial smells. I felt as if Ravin was hiding himself in perfumed air around him and not letting me know his original smell.

I wanted fresh air which is a crime in Indian occasions. He tried to kiss my lips which were highlighted by a deep rosy red lipstick. I was already prepared for that moment.

"Don't you have trust on me yet? After engagement also," I said. "Have patience, *yaar*. I'm all yours now. Where will I go?"

"Shama, don't worry about Uncle. I mean Dad, now. Nothing will happen to him," he said.

He predicted the reason for my continuous denial of kissing. He had been observing my glances to my Dad during the ceremony. But actually I was not ready to accept Ravin with any foreign smell around us.

After that, he didn't try to touch me. He introduced me to almost all members of his family. I believe I had acted perfectly for showing my interest to know them well. Perhaps due to marriage seemed as long distanced thing. He looked happy when I gently kissed the engagement ring when they were leaving. I think I had made that gesture due to my habit of making him happy always in the last moment.

20.

Next day, when I reached my hostel, gate keeper told me that an auto-rickshaw driver had been coming every morning to meet me. I regretted I forgot that kind man. He came again and I paid him back his money.

“Sorry, I had to visit my home urgently,” I said.

“It’s ok. Did you manage things at police station that day?” he asked.

“Yes yes, everything was done in five hundred rupees only. I can’t imagine what would have happened if you didn’t help me.”

He left and I moved towards my department. In the practical session, I saw Sid chatting with his fan club for the first time. First time during his practicals. His fans were insisting him for something I couldn’t figure out. I started to put on white apron and blue hand gloves. He came to his work place near me and seemed like he had no lab work.

"Have you seen the girl in last *fair and lovely* advertisement?" he said.

"Maybe. I don't see ads so carefully," I said, closing big white buttons of my apron.

"Why are you jealous of other girls' beauty?"

"I am not jealous. Tell me who do remember ads?"

"You will see her in movies shortly. She is such a beauty."

"I have nothing to do with movies."

"Then who did go to see *Veer-Zaara*?" he said. I thought he was reaching on point now.

"What do you want me to say? I am burning from that advertisement girl. Ok? I said it. Happy?"

"Chill. Chill. I can notice you have done a profitable deal of your beauty. How was the engagement?"

"Who told you that?" I asked in astonishing voice.

"No one."

"Then?"

"I can see light brown hue of your *mahendi* color palms. And ring is also there on your third finger. Isn't it?" he said. I wondered how he could catch it as I was wearing hand gloves.

He went on telling me.

"You did engagement in such a hurry, you didn't bother much about your face. My sharp eyes can spot your moustache. Hahaha! Boys of my age don't have eyes. We have binoculars when we are looking at girl of our age. But for me, I don't have binoculars. I have X-ray machines which can scan up to..."

"Shut up now, Sid."

"Oh! How good it feels when you speak my nick name. By the way, now as you are engaged, you have very less time for flirting. After marriage…" he said.

"How good will you feel if I use my hand again on your cheek?"

"Let's go to the library. Padmini Madam is also not there in her cabin. I don't have anything to do today. And why are you wearing this apron? No one is working today. Today at 4 o'clock, there will be an oratory competition in the auditorium. Don't you know?"

Now I understood, his fan club might be insisting him to perform in competition.

I put off my apron and hand gloves. We both sat at the same place we used to in the library.

"I really like when you follow whatever I insist," he said.

"When did I follow you?"

"Just now I told you to be fast for flirting. And see, we are here. Alone..." he said, scanning me by his binocular kind of eyes.

"You can think whatever you want to. Why should I control your thoughts?" I said.

"By the way, engagement seems like bondage but it actually gives freedom. What you say?" he said.

"I don't understand you. What do you want to say?"

"Ravin is in this building. May be he could be in his lab. It is quite possible that he can see us alone here. I don't think you have thought of this."

I immediately felt weight of being engaged. I took back my *mahendi* colored hand which was just two inches away from Sid's hands on the table.

"Ravin is not a kind of guy you are thinking," I said, trying to look normal. I had to save Ravin's image to save mine.

Sid stood up and opened two scientific journals. He kept one of them in front of me and one in front of him.

"If he comes now, we can have good excuse," he said. I pretended as if it was not much necessary for me.

"Let's talk about real thing please," I suggested.

"Oh! Another discussion of sex and love," he said.

"No. The real thing, *yaar*. I can't believe that you have written that story of tree and child."

"Lot of people sent me letters asking that question. I don't answer them," he said.

"Why? Because you haven't written it?"

"No. Because they don't deserve answer from me," he said.

"How can you say that?"

"I am showing you moon and you people are catching my finger I am pointing towards it. I am telling you what is love and you, investigative officers, are busy in finding from where I copied the story."

He was quite right. I was among those investigative officers. That story touched my heart but very soon my thoughts were focusing on the story teller Sid. How many times I told myself, "Sid can't write such a story. He can only write those erotic ones."

"But at least you should answer if I ask you the question which is in between us. Why did you lie that Ravin had written a letter to HOD about my detention?" I said.

"Yes, this is right question. You should be the investigative officer to find it out. Do you know what happened today morning? I, by myself, met Ravin to inform him why I lied. But he was not interested to know. He showed me his engagement ring and said he wanted you and he got. He felt like winning because I was creating trouble for him even though he got you. I congratulated him and came back," Sid said.

"You are not answering anything and just making meaningless circles. Well, tell me how Avni looks like?"

"She has some lines similar to that *fair and lovely* advertisement girl. But, I predict she will be look like Padmini Madam when she will reach in her forties," he said.

"Do you meet her still?"

"Of course. I met her just yesterday. Actually, I need her the most these days."

"May I know for what?"

"I am preparing for the third cassette. I need her voice for some part of recording."

"Why her, particularly? Can't you give me a chance?"

"You? No no. You can't give justice to the story of this time. It's a new angle of Draupadi's story."

"So what? Why can't I give justice?"

"Avni is closer to Draupadi's character."

"How?"

"She had five boyfriends at a time as Draupadi had five husbands together. And you? You know yourself better."

I felt like I am terribly missing something to join Sid in his third cassette project.

Before I would think any other problem in me, he said something which shocked me deeply and it dragged whole of my mind.

"There is an amazing word in Urdu. *Raqeeb*. Do you know the meaning of *Raqeeb*?"

"No."

"If two boys love the same girl then both boys are *Raqeeb* of each other. No other language has taken care to develop a word for such a relationship," he said.

"Ok. So what?"

"I and Ravin were *Raqeeb* of each other," he said. "We both were among those five boyfriends of Avni."

I expected the familiar lines of teasing on his face but there were none. I waited for around half a minute keeping my eyes down. The silent time passed was enough to confirm the news. I closed the journal and left with fuming face.

"We all are still in her touch but she broke up with all of us together," he kept giving me information.

When I reached the gate of library, he ran fast and caught me. He picked me up in her arms. My struggles to free me from him were in vain. My nostrils had no options other than his body smell. He brought me back to our place at library. He spread me on the table as if I was table cloth. I saw a ceiling fan moving slowly over me. He sat both of his elbows on sides of my neck and said, "Just tell me what you were going to do with your fiancé?"

"Even in the engagement," I said in regretting voice, "I was feeling like he was hiding something. I can't be with such a fraud."

"I think you should marry him," Sid said. "You have the primary quality for becoming wife. You want to seize him. You didn't care to confirm whether there is any truth or not. How often I did lie to you? Even though you believed me instantly. Why?"

I kept looking at him and thinking. He took back his hands from around my neck and said, "I was just befooling you. Now, let's move to the igloo. I am going to perform on today's education in my view."

He left. I was rubbing my engagement ring with index finger. Suddenly I felt a discomfort due to tightness of the ring. I wished to free my finger for a while. But not forever.

21.

In the igloo, no one from Sid's huge fan club could tell him to go on the mike as Shardul Sir, Padmini Madam and another retired professor had already took their seats before Sid came. Everyone knew that Sid had participated and most of us were eager to hear him.

That day, Ravin sat in the first row. I sat in seventh raw where my regular seat was, in the girl's section. He found me easily and when we saw each other, he kissed his engagement ring. He kept doing it until I reacted in the same way, but with an artificial smile. I regretted I had invented that way of showing love. He had just copied my gesture I did when we were parting after our engagement.

Actually I didn't like igloo's atmosphere. Maybe because, the new peon had spread *Natura*'s lemon air freshener. Again, an artificial smell.

In their speech, all participants criticized contemporary education for issues of donations, old syllabus, poor practical approach etc. They said today's education is not the real one. Sid's turn was last. While walking towards the stage, he checked his pant's zip. He started and very soon he sky-rocketed our minds.

"Now, when we are about to reach out our destination, people are telling, O boy… the long way of sea you just passed, was not the sea." Whole auditorium laughed on it.

"Then what is it? If it was not sea, what was it? I had been boating from so many years and now I am standing in front of the destination and they say it was not the sea. Come, dive inside and see whether it's the sea or not?"

Sid pointed a finger towards another participant who criticized the present education system. Everyone supported Sid as he was giving what was expected from him. "Was it a joke happening with us since so many years? We are studying from last seventeen years, these Ph.D. fellows from twenty one years, and now these people are telling all that we did is not education. I was reading till midnights, where did all that gone? Is that meaningless now? If all this present education is meaningless, then which one is right one?"

"We saw an archery education in Mahabharata, is that meaningful today? Raise your hand who wants to learn archery." No hands were raised. "Who needs it now? See, no one. What we need to learn is how to make *Paracetamol*? Tell me. Will we massage our father's head if he would have headache? No. We will give him one rupee *Paracetamol*. Take it and sleep. We are getting the education what we need and that is the only true education."

"And why? Why some people are against fees? Fees were always there. Earlier it was called *Gurudakshina*. That's it. *Eklavya* gave his thumb as *Gurudakshina*. Will we give? No. We will pay money instead. That was the time when Guru *Drona* invented tuition classes for special education to children of king *Dhrutrashtra*. Now we have self-financed quota for rich. Just another version of it. Isn't it? In short, today's education is the education only, nothing else."

"If this is not education, then what is the difference between us and those illiterate laborers digging outside?"

Now listen to the last thing. We all are about to register our names at marriage bureau. Isn't it? We have to write we are postgraduates of Chemistry and bla bla bla. Parents of eligible candidates will be attracted towards our photo-shopped picture and ask, "How much he or she is educated?" At that time, our parents will have a nice answer. "M.Sc." Master-blaster of science. Then only life will go on. Isn't it? What say? Thank you."

His fan club couldn't control their emotions. Whole igloo had been filled with the echoes of "Sidhuuu… Sidhu… Sidhuuu… Sidhuu….!"

22.

I wouldn't have taken Sid's suggestion of being investigative officer seriously if I didn't see him with Padmini Madam in a questionable gesture.

On that day, I had left my hostel earlier than regular. I thought I would be in beauty parlor for around forty five minutes and then move to the department. I reached there and read a notice on the dilapidated iron shutter of the parlor.

"Parlor will be opened after two days."

I knew that library always opens one hour before the department. So, I decided to reach there and start reading as our internal exam was just after a week. I hadn't prepared enough for passing the exam because my study lazy mind had reasonable excuses of my engagement and that fire incident.

But now, I had made up my mind to focus on studying only. It was a new thing for me to make a time table to study and follow it. While moving towards the library, I passed by Padmini Madam's personal research lab. As expected, her cabin's main door was open. It was a known fact that she starts working early in the morning. A happy and manly voice coming out from her lab grabbed my attention. It took time to recognize whose voice it was.

I couldn't expect Sid to be with Padmini Madam. Alone. Before the department's working hours. Particularly because Madam had already closed doors of her cabin for Sid after we got "C grade" from NAAC.

"Aaah..." Sid was telling in a tired voice as if he would be stretching his body. "I loved it."

I had clearly caught these words. I slowly stepped towards the door little more and pressed it as gently as no noise came out. I saw Madam had sat on her big table besides her computer. Her legs were hanging, moving forward and backward like pendulum. She kept up her hand with open palm as if she is inviting Sid to clap on it. Sid did it instantly. They clapped like winners. Madam's celebrity smile had become permanent. And Sid was the only one to be entertained there. Then suddenly she jumped from the table and hugged him tightly. My eye muscles had no energy to see more. I left for library and tried to focus my study but failed. I imagined most of the physical positions between them which Sid narrated in her dirty audio stories. My mind had completed that unfinished tattoo on the bicep of Sid. "X-Sangeeta, Y-Avni, Z-Padmini"

I entered my classroom with the decision to investigate the reality of Sid.

There was Shardul Sir's lecture. So, Sid placed her bag on the first bench. The first button of his shirt was open. Sir was just entering in the classroom and Sid was leaving. As always, when they crossed, Sid greeted him "Good morning, Sir" and Sir didn't reply. He couldn't forget reason for C grade.

I took Sid's bag and sat on my place. After the prayer, whenever Sir got busy at the black board, I kept checking Sid's bag.

First thing I found was a walkman on which "record" button was pressed. I didn't switch it off. Both visible circles were circling over, which means, recording was on. Suddenly I understood why Sid was keeping his bag on the first bench of classroom. To have all the information about whatever was going on in the class. Now I got how he had the information that Shardul Sir had announced the quiz the other day.

The second thing was a white open envelope. I checked inside it- Two flight tickets from Vadodara to Goa. I imagined Padmini Madam in bikini and Sid in short cloths, sleeping on the long wooden benches, at Candolim beach of Goa. Date mentioned on tickets was after the internal exam. No other suspicious things I could find.

23.

In that internal exam, I didn't need to do indirect request to Ravin for help. He understood it without saying. Being his fiancée, it was my right to have benefit of his position and power. I studied up to my capacity and remembered whatever I could keep in my table tennis ball sized mind. I had studied for internal exam with half mind as other half was busy to investigate the thing between Sid and Madam. I couldn't help myself.

What could be more interesting than exploring controversial relationships of others?

Ravin was present as a liberal supervisor for two papers. For another two papers, he settled his other colleagues who ignored micro Xerox chits of mine and my long glances at nearby answer sheets. I confirm that I wanted to show my Dad that I had taken a step to make a life. To see some lines of satisfaction on my dying Dad, I could do anything. Using relations, cheating, just anything on the earth!

On the last day of my internal exam, when the last bell rang, I had a confidence that I would be passed in all subjects with average marks. A strange kind of luckiness I felt for being fiancée of Ravin.

"What would happen if I won't be engaged to Ravin?" I told myself.

But, that help was not free. I had to pay for it. After exams over, I didn't have reason to save myself from being touched by him.

He had already booked two tickets for movie. He took me to watch movie. He started kissing me as lights off immediately after national anthem. His way of kissing reminded me of a thing once told by Sid. Sid had a girlfriend whose mouth took shape as if there was a *pani-puri* inside. I laughed. Ravin didn't like it but he kept kissing my lips. He started making much sound as if one is licking honey on porcelain tea dish.

Thank god, two old couples were sat in next raw behind us. They complained when Ravin's kissing sound reached to their ears.

"O hello! Don't make such sounds. Let others focus on the movie," said an old man. "Better you understand before my wife open her mouth. She can abuse anyone continuously for one minute without repeating a single word."

Ravin pretended as if he was not feared and moved back. But, I pressed his hand and stopped him.

"No no Ravi," I said. "They are elders. Let's see the movie now."

It was a boring movie. But, I liked it.

24.

For two days after our internal exam, I couldn't find Sid and Padmini Madam in the department. Then, I saw Sid was entering in the lab for our practical session. I predicted they had a good quality time at Candolim beach of Goa. I wondered that he was in no hurry for work. He seemed as if he just came for visit. He was strolling carefree and enjoying as if he is in the garden. There was a mischievous smile on his paan-reddish lips.

He came to me and said, "Good good. You have started investigation."

I hide my astonishment, smiled and said, "You are bigger investigator. How do you know that I have started investigation?"

I asked him even though I knew the answer. May be he would reveal something I couldn't catch.

"I was listening to the recorded cassette I always hide in my bag. Shardul Sir's voice was little lower than usual. So, I thought you might have checked my bag and kept it with you on your last bench for whole lecture. Isn't it?" he said.

Before I would ask him anything about those two flight tickets, we saw Padmini Madam came out of her cabin and threw a glance at Sid. Sid rubbed his tongue on upper lips and said to me, "I am coming after making her happy."

He immediately started walking towards her cabin as if there would be any fire to be extinguished. He came back after half an hour. He was closing his first upper button of the shirt.

"So, when are you completing your tattoo by Z-Padmini?" I asked. Finally I dared to announce the result of my investigation.

"You reminded me well. Very soon I will do it. You are really good investigator. I am sure you had seen our flight tickets for Goa. It was amazing. My first flight!! By the way, how was your exams this time?" he said.

I wondered why he wasn't surprised at all.

"Better. By the way, I couldn't understand why you keep recording Shardul Sir's lecture? You can easily get notes from anyone instead of recording," I said.

"Most of our syllabi don't need much understanding. Our education system checks memory only. So, I just keep listening recorded cassettes and memorize. Before last day of exam, I adjust them question-answer wise and you see most of the time, I emerge as topper. I just focus well on practical on regular days," he said.

I thought this man earned everything by walkman only. I couldn't believe that the creator of tree & child's story and this dirty character man are the same.

Padmini Madam came out of her cabin again and said, "All of you, come this side."

"I have invited Lupin pharma for campus interview here. They will conduct your interviews next week. Be prepared for tough questions. And most importantly, at least don't ruin my reputation in front of them. You may not know I was manager in Lupin R&D before joining here, this C grade department. All the best!" She announced and went back.

We all cheered up for that shining possibility. Everyone had lost hope of campus interview after she got angry when department was awarded C grade. No one could understand this sudden change of her.

"I think only you know what made change her mind. Are you behind that? I mean she was not at all interested in arranging campus interview for us," I asked Sid.

"I told you I am going inside to make her happy," he said.

"Please Sid. Seriously!"

"Again same problem is with you. You have superb opportunity to make your life but you are interested in knowing why it is happening," he said and again he was quite right.

"If you promise me that you will not ask any more questions and focus on preparation of campus interview, then only I will tell you what made her change her mind."

I agreed.

"I always knew that she is interested in my proposal of cost effective synthesis of *Viagra*. One day, when I emailed her my progress on that project, she got impressed and started helping me for chemicals and other utilities. I got succeed to develop a process which can be patented as a new chemical process. Just one step, one very important step was remained. Testing of it on living organism. She helped me to do it in Concord biopharma Lab at Goa. After our exam, we both went there and did it. Actually she did it. She knew how to do it. She also taught me there. Now I and she are going to apply for patent shortly. It will be such a big achievement that based on it, department can get A+ grade. No department from whole Gujarat ever got succeed for a single patent. I kept requesting her for arranging campus interview. But she said that I should not think of others. According to her, most of us are stupid," said Sid and checked whether others were eavesdropping our discussion or not. Then, he went on.

"Today, I told her, "I had great news. I can only tell you if you promise me to invite at least one company for campus interview. She agreed. I said, "Swami Sir is promoted to chairman of UGC. I think there will be no hurdles for "A+" grade in next NAAC visit which is after six months. We also may have patent on our name as a credit. But, the most important reason will be my absence in the department. Hopefully I will be selected in campus interview you are going to arrange now."

Suddenly, I felt a kind of respect for Sid. A kind of respect that happens when one knows the truth after a long term negative thinking for somebody.

"Do you know what I was thinking about you and Madam?" I said.

"Of course I know. Actually, I was checking you," he said.

"What? What checking me?"

"I make a person of my need. But in my last two efforts, there might be some fault in my making. You know Sangi and Avni left me. I think I haven't made any mistake in shaping you. You are almost ready to be in relationship with me," he said.

I wished he would be in his old teasing mood. But he was not.

"I don't think you have changed me in any way? I am going to marry Ravin. Don't you know?" I argued.

"When marriage can be broken, what is the value of engagement?" he said. I couldn't agree or disagree with him.

"But what could you do when you realize that you had made some mistake in making someone?" I asked.

"I leave or they leave me like Sangeeta and Anvi. But that experience makes me better maker. See Avni was better than Sangi and you will be better than Avni," he said.

"You please forget me, Sid. And don't you think two persons should learn to adjust with each other rather than changing partners every season?"

"No. Up to when we can improve, why do we adjust?" he said. "I don"t agree with the popular belief that as the number of relationships are more, person is bad. No. It's not necessary. Nelson Mandela and Salman Rushdie married thrice. Aren't they amazing people? Rushdie is still in his 70's and in fully working condition. His fourth marriage is quite possible. Isn't it? I think marriages should have an expiry date. Maximum five years," he said.

I never heard the names he was mentioning. "Sorry, world can't afford your ideology," I said.

"Yes. It's too expensive for your poor world," he said with the pride of rich people.

25.

Next day, we all saw the written notice of campus interview in the notice board. The newly printed paper was fixed besides the old notification of "C grade" award. HR department of Lupin Pharma had also provided a glossy paper print which had a green flower logo, vision of the company and a special program named.

"YLP- Young Leaders Program has been designed to identify and attract the best talent from technical campuses, in order to build a talent pipeline in the company."

In the back ground, as a watermark, there was a picture of highly equipped R&D lab which was the work place in dreams of most of us.

Suddenly our classroom had been filled with the air of shining possibilities. Everyone was busy in getting prepared well for campus interview. All were imagining to call home after a week and say, "Yes papa, I am selected under Young Leaders Program as an executive for R&D in Lupin."

Boys, who had been used to wear T-shirts and sports shoes, bought full sleeves plain color shirt and formal black shoes. Some girls tried zero power glasses to look decent and studious. No one was showing their format of CV to others. All entered into the mentality of defeating others.

I daydreamed about calling my dad. "I am joining Lupin, Dad, I have taken a step to make a life," I was telling him.

But I got really waked up for preparation of interview when I saw my classmates with print outs of their CVs. I hadn't made it yet. I reached a cyber café, sat in a closed wooden compartment, searched some latest CV formats and prepared one for me. When I ordered for its print, I saw Sid at the counter.

I saw a print out in his hand and asked, "Hey Sid, may I see your CV?"

"This is not CV. But you can see it," he said and gave me a paper. It was the script of his third cassette.

"Oh! Third one is in process! May I read it?"

"Yes. By the way, a lot of things are yet to be added to this. But it's ok. You can read it now."

I went back to wooden compartment and started reading it.

"In swayamvar of Draupadi, Arjun took hold of the bow, stringed it, gazed at the reflecting pool and hit an eye of the target fish. He had won the hand of Draupadi. He and his other four brothers - Yudhisthir, Bheema, Sahdev and Nakul, reached their house where their mother was staying. They announced their coming with the words, "Mother, we have brought a prize."

Mother Kunti was inside the house and didn't see them. As usual she said, "All of you can share whatever you have brought."

With that they all married Draupadi.

My dear listeners, Is it possible?

When mother would have known that they meant Draupadi when they said prize, couldn't she say, "Oh, sorry sorry, I didn't know that you came up with a young girl."

It was just a small misunderstanding which can be easily cleared. It's impossible that just mother told and they followed it literally without any second thought. What would you have done if you would be Arjun?

Yet if you believe that their conversation was practical, then please, off your walkman. You are not capable to digest my thoughts. Go read Mayapuri, Chitrlok whatever.

Actually, somehow Kunti already had information that her sons had come up with Draupadi. Draupadi was the most beautiful and glamorous girl of that era. Swayamvar was a big expensive event which couldn't be arranged for any ordinary girl. She was so desirable that she could be a reason of a war in between five Pandvas which was originally fought between Kauravas and Pandvas.

Like every mother, Kunti knew her sons. It was due to her foresight that she suggested sharing of that prize. She felt much discomfort for her words. Obviously! How can a woman suggest to another woman to be a wife of her five sons?

And then what happened? Draupadi was a 'thing', which was won by someone's archery skill. The society never gives a freedom of speech to a thing. She was a newly wedded and won thing, couldn't raise a voice against mother-son's collective decision.

I predict how her night time would be shared by five brothers.

Monday - Arjun, because he won her. Without him, she would not be there.

Tuesday - Yudhisthir, because he was the eldest brother.

Wednesday - Bheem, because he was a blood brother of Arjun and Yudhisthir.

Thursday - Sahdev, because he was elder to Nakul.

Friday - Nakul.

Saturday, Sunday - holiday, Five days a week!

I personally believe that Friday would be the favorite day of Draupadi. All job doing people love Friday because after Friday, they can have two days long holiday from work.

Nakul would be her most favorite person out of five. He was the most handsome amongst all five. And one more solid reason is that she could easily see the similarity of her situation with his. As a youngest brother, Nakul always got whatever had been left after his four brothers. This time also, he had got a left thing after use, Draupadi.

Life had given very less to Nakul and Draupadi. Even though, both of them had physical beauty, they didn't have freedom to feel proud on it. They had their own little private pleasures. Only Nakul could see her in her most happy time, Friday, because her eyes couldn't hide her happiness of long holiday of Saturday Sunday. How could she hide it? Imagine yourself as inexperienced Draupadi who had been rubbed under experienced athletic thighs. Yes. They had their personal wives also, other than Draupadi.

After over introduction of five different bodies, no wonder if her heart would have been attracted towards much higher spirit. Friendship. The five weren't able to become her friends. Rarely any husband can become a friend of his wife. She found a genuine friendship in Krishna. Actually, only due to Krishna's friendship, there would be some respect for the man's being in her sight.

Whom she called in the tragic moment when Duryodhan was removing her clothes in open court? Those were the friendship's ears which could hear Draupadi's call. Only friendship's hands came to help her there.

In fact, she could live without long holidays also as she had a person who listened to her pain, happiness, desires and memories. Krishna's ability to connect with her was unique. During conversations, he always kept asking little questions; about details of any event she was sharing, to show that he is absorbing her talk with full attention. That arrangement of sharing a pain by words to someone's ears was keeping her alive and convincing to love the life.

My dear listeners, love's good bad experiences are just steps to reach higher spirit. Friendship. Friendship is the pinnacle of love's mountain."

I couldn't stand up. I kept touching letters on the print. I felt like crying.

Sid opened that small wooden door and said, "Done? How is it?"

I tried to speak some words but only few unclear words came out. A drop of tear fell on that print. He helped me to stand up. I stood up, hugged him tightly. I cleaned my tears and wet running nose on his shoulder.

When I was paying for my CV's print, Sid said, "I think we can dub it in your voice."

"Why?" I asked, "Is Avni not ready?"

"I haven't asked her yet. Don't need her now. I think I have made you much better." I tried hard to hide my excitement and nodded.

"So when will we dub?" he asked.

"After campus interview," I answered.

"After getting selected," he corrected my words with confidence.

I thought he was just saying it to be nice. I have no reason to keep confidence about my selection. He has. He was able.

26.

Padmini Madam conducted an extra lecture to give us some important information about campus interview. She didn't throw her celebrity smile. She didn't look happy with our opportunity. I thought she was arranging campus interview just because Sid changed her mind a little. She directly came to the point.

"HR manager called me to convey some information to you before they visit us. See, the top executives in Lupin are going to retire together after seven to eight years. So, company wants to hire fresh talents who may work for that many years with them and then take positions of retired executives. They will tell you to sign the officially legal bond spanning at least five years if you will get selected under YLP. It means you can't leave the company before that duration."

"After five years, no one will leave job because just after two more years, you would be in the top rank executive category. In short, their idea is that if young talents join their company, then company can have top authorities on time in future."

"In interview, answer their questions only if you know surely. Otherwise pass it. Please don't brainstorm instantly and throw any stupid answer. Just remember that I have a big reputation there. Don't let my name down. Those who don't want the job, please avoid interview. And there by help the really interested ones."

"Last thing, even if you get selected, you must have first class as average of all four semesters. If you couldn't score it, your selection will be cancelled automatically. So, don't be careless about study even after your selection."

Madam disappointed me with that last condition of first class. First time I calculated an average of my three semester's result. I had to score 88% in that final semester to achieve first class average. It was impossible to score it with my table tennis ball sized memory.

She had broken my imagination of calling home and making disappointingly dying Dad a happily dying Dad. But, I was so charged that I could see a possibility. I thought I must try to get selected. If Dad will die in between my selection and final semester's result, he would die happily. He would never know that my selection would be cancelled after not fulfilling first class average condition. By any means, I wanted to show my Dad some good time before his death.

I had made my mind to prepare myself as much as possible. I never became so studious before the announcement of campus interview. Firstly, I started to clear my concepts whichever I found my cup of tea. As I kept going, I regretted that I never studied with interest. I learned some tips to face interview from internet. I prayed to god regularly for that week. Just before a day of interview, I made a mistake.

Ravin had come to the gate of my hostel to meet me.

"Can you take me to a market? I need to buy a decent pant-shirt," I said to Ravin.

I never had that kind of clothes. I never went out of my strategy of using beauty as weapon and believing in my mother's saying, "Beauty is in simplicity."

"Why do suddenly you get interested in that kind of dressing?" he said.

"We will have a campus interview tomorrow. Don't you know?"

"So, what?"

"What? I am preparing so much to appear. I couldn't find time to go and buy. I just kept delaying and see, today is the last day," I said.

"I will buy it for you if you like it but you are not going to appear in the interview."

"I want to appear, Ravi."

"I am enough to earn, Shama, you will never have to work. Even you too wanted to rest under the shadow of my tree. Isn't it?"

I saw the lines of stubbornness on his face. I smelled bad in spite of he came first time without sprinkling any perfume. He was quite right but I didn't like the way he reminded me. I definitely wanted him for my long term future but in my near future, I wanted to get selected for job. Thank god, I hadn't informed Ravin that I was all prepared to dub my voice in Sid's third cassette. Only god knows how would he react on hearing that?

"Ravi, I want to face interview just for fun. Most of my classmates are appearing. Also, that company requires students having first class average which is not possible for me. So, there are no real chances. And don't you know my knowledge? Do you think I can be selected?" I said.

I don't know which emotions were on my face. Was I happy with me? Or disappointed? But looking at him, I knew I had just done an undeniable argument. He had no reason to stop me from having fun. That so-called fun to face interview.

He took me happily to the nearest Westside store. I chose pant shirt quickly. I avoided asking him for the review of my look in those clothes.

"Let's buy some western clothes for you," he said and started suggesting some short clothes, one after another.

I pretended to look happy. Inside, I was planning to get back to my room as early as possible and revise whatever I had prepared for interview. I came back with newly bought formals of my choice and two western pieces of Ravin's choice.

27.

I had decided to not call my home and inform my parents about campus interview. I thought that if anyhow I would be selected, then only I would call and inform my Dad.

Finally the day came; I got ready with my unimpressive CV and mark sheets, sober look with my pant-shirt, some clear concepts of Chemistry and ongoing prayers in my heart. Ravin had come to my hostel's gate again even though I hadn't told him to bring me to the department.

"Oh baby!" he said touching my checks shirt's shoulder, "You are looking like an interviewer."

I sat on the back seat of his bike and my nostrils filled with strong acidic smell of his new perfume. During the ride, I kept inhaling less and exhaling with force. Up to when he had been parking, I had left him hurriedly with words, "I think we are little late." In fact we were on time.

I had never faced any kind of interview before. But I had been appeared for viva voce three times in last three semesters. Mostly I hadn't answered in viva voce. And whenever I answered, I spoke with much low confidence. I always felt the viva voce room, suffocating even though there were two 1.5 ton capacity air conditioners running inside. I didn't like it when I knew that our viva voce room had been allotted for Lupin's campus interview.

In the big hall in front of the viva vice room, we all, well dressed candidates were waiting for our turns.

I noticed Sid. He was the only one in Jeans and T shirt. All other boys were in formal clothes and resembling Ravin who used to be look like private bank employee without tie. Most of my classmates, even Sid's fan club, would have liked his silly dressing.

Who doesn't like when a strong competitor weakens himself?

Sid was chewing *paan* and seemed careless about the interview. He came to me and sat on the next chair. I inhaled relaxing smell of *qimam*. I felt as if Sid's careless attitude would be spreading inside me. I filled the smell in my lungs and kept as long as I could.

Interviews had been started. No one was revealing about what kind of questions were being asked inside the room. If anyone was revealing, he was trying to misguide others. Some of us had read some psychologist's tips to break other's confidence. When such candidates came out of interview room, they were telling he was selected by the interview panel. Just to break other's confidence. What else?

Sid's turn came. He went inside with some printed papers in his hands. He didn't even bother to keep a file of documents. I heard some gossips about him there.

"If he wants to do Ph.D. under Madam, why do he appearing in campus? Sick mentality. What else? He is just reducing our chances."

"You see, they will kick him out in a minute. These corporate people don't like such unprofessional behavior. Hahah!! Who wears jeans T-shirt for appearing in interview? How can he come as if he is visiting garden?"

I thought that gossips had some truth when I saw Sid was coming out from viva voce room after finishing interview in just exactly one minute. Lot of waiting faces smiled. He directly pointed his forefinger to me and said, "You go inside."

I hurriedly saw myself in the glass of my wrist watch and started walking towards viva voce room. When I was about to cross Sid, he caught my wrist and his lips were whispering in my ears.

"If you want to get selected, just say "yes" to their first question. And then, answer other questions as if I would have been answering from your tongue. Understood?"

I was over alert. I absorbed his instruction. That relaxing smell of *qimam* coming out from his mouth convinced me to trust him.

"Yes ok," I said.

There was no time to think about what exactly was going on with me. I entered the chilled room where two middle aged persons in black suits were sat.

"May I come in, Sir?"

One of them nodded. I sat on the chair in front of them.

"So, are you going to marry Siddharth?" one of them asked.

"Yes," I answered. Part of my mind started investigating what was happening.

"Congratulations," he said.

"Thanks," I said and smiled but a little. I read Lupin's identity card hanging on his tie- "Mr. Sujoy Ghosh, Senior Manager HR"

Another person, who had oversized glasses and sharply shaped mustache, had an identity card with words, "Dr. D A Vaishnav, Manager R & D"

"Tell me what frankness is? According to you," Sujoy Sir asked.

I knew that now I should be answering as if I was Sid.

"When a girl sneezes, wipes nose or even yawns, she says sorry. But not when she farts. One should take responsibility and say sorry for every mistake. No point of shying away of anything. That is frankness," I said.

Both serious faces in front of me relaxed instantly and they laughed so much. Vaishnav Sir was laughing without voice. But his whole heavy body was moving. Especially shoulders were moving up and down. He forwarded his one hand for clap with Sujoy Sir. They clapped.

"See Miss," Sujoy Sir checked my name in a paper, "Miss Shama, frankness is a must quality to work in R & D. Our R & D's aim is to develop medicines for current burning health problems. There will be discussions on human sexuality, *Viagra*, menstruation cycle, menopause etc. If our young leaders would be a shy person, how can she discuss openly? So, who are you? Are you shy or frank? If you are frank, prove it."

"Sir, I am frank. But I am not having nature whisper right now, so don't know how to prove my frankness," I said.

"Nature's whisper? What is it?" they asked together, looking at each other.

"If we say the feeling of urinate or defecate as nature call, can't we say farting as nature whisper?" I said.

Again Vaishnav Sir's shoulders started moving. Sujoy Sir noted something on his paper. I found myself in Sid's careless attitude. I didn't try to see what he was writing.

"Our company has twelve locations over India. Suppose you and Siddharth are married and got selected under our YLP, and we locate you both in two different cities very far from each other, how will you manage?" asked Sujoy Sir, adjusting his HR manager's identity card.

"Sir, under YLP, you are hiring young people. But youngness is not just for our working hours in company. Young people need to relax their sexual tension time to time. If it would not be done, they can't focus well at their work place. So, in fact, this hypothetical question checks your intentions. Not mine."

I realized that I had just revealed something from mind which was originally told in Sid's second cassette.

"This institute is awarded "C grade" by NAAC. Yet, we are conducting campus interview here. We could go to the IITs. Don't you think you people are lucky?" said Sujoy Sir.

"No, Sir."

"Why?"

"Because you are hiring people, not institutes. If you identify well, you can have young talents from here also. If you don't, you will not have them from even IIT or Oxford. Actually one should make or train person of his requirement. Not just choose any stupid from available mass. As I have shaped Siddharth to be a person of my need."

I said but I knew I was answering on behalf of Sid. I had just exchanged our names. Truth was Sid had shaped up me.

Sujoy Sir gave me an offer letter having Lupin's green flower logo.

"Read it and sign, if you agree," he said.

I hurriedly read validity of offer, training period, stipend, leave, notice period and joining date. The last line was hand written and signed by Sid. It dragged my whole attention.

"We undersigned, Shama and Siddharth will marry before joining the company as executives recruited under YLP."

I confirm that I hadn't predicted any consequences during signing and thanking them. I just imagined some lines of satisfaction on my Dad's face. They were reflecting on my face when I was calling him from a yellow STD booth.

Finally Vaishnav Sir shook hands with me and said, "I hope you both score much higher in this final semester, get happily married. So, this offer letter could retain its meaning."

I clearly got his meaning. He was reminding me the condition of first class average. That distanced worry was nothing in front of my near joy of calling home and telling my Dad, "Yes Dad, I am going to join Lupin R & D next July."

28.

Later Sid told me about what had happened in the viva voce room with him. When he entered, looking at his dressing, Vaishnav Sir said, "Do you think such clothes are suitable to appear in company job interview?

"Sir, interview means interviewer will try to know me from my inside. It has nothing to do with my outside. Isn't it?" said Sid.

Vaishnav Sir looked at Sujoy Sir and said, "I think this boy want to be handled by HR. But let me first check him for technical knowledge."

Sujoy Sir nodded.

Before Vaishnav Sir started asking anything, Sid said, "Sir, if you ask me any question of Chemistry and perhaps I would answer correctly, it would be mere my luck. You may have asked me which I readily read somewhere. Even I can ask you some questions and guarantee that you can't answer. So please, give me a minute and you will be able to take decision about me within no time."

Sid stood with logic and they agreed to give him a minute. They were thinking that there would be no difficulty in rejecting this over smart boy.

"See, this is the short draft of patent for cost effective synthesis of *Viagra*. I and Padmini Madam are going to submit it by end of this month."

Sid gave a paper to Vaishnav Sir and said, "Sir, I know Lupin want to have cost reduction of his *Viagra* plant by any means. I don't need to explain that this patent have too high chances to be accepted. You know Padmini Madam is involved in this. If I am not wrong, she was on the same position in Lupin where you are now."

Sid looked at Vaishnav Sir.

"If you are selecting me, I will be trying with full heart for scale up the method I and Madam have developed."

By then, Vaishnav Sir had reviewed and understood the potential of patent draft. He nodded looking at Sujoy Sir.

"One more thing, Sir. You obviously know that such things may take long time and dedication. I am keenly interested to be in Lupin under YLP and ready to sign legal bond of any duration you say. I can only join Lupin if you select my fiancée also, because we both want to have a happy family and a job to focus on our project. She is also my classmate. If we both will be together, YLP's aim will also be supported automatically. There will be no reason to leave Lupin in future. Have a look at my mark sheets also," Sid said and showed his three semester's mark sheet. He impressed them with it too.

"You are invited to Lupin but we have to interview your fiancée. We can't just offer her the job because she is in your relationship," said Sujoy Sir.

"As I told you, Sir. Asking technical questions is meaningless. I insist you to check her for her intellectual clarity. You will be surely satisfied," Sid said.

They agreed.

"What if you don't marry her?" Vaishnav Sir said suddenly.

"After I leave from here, I will send her inside. As and when she would come, you may ask her for confirmation of our marriage. If she denies, you can cancel my offer and interview her by your own way." said Sid.

"Ok Siddharth," Sujoy Sir said, "Let's do one thing. You write that you both are going to marry on this offer letter I am giving you. If we will find her with high intellectual clarity, we will select her and take her signature on this same offer letter. If we will find her unable, your offer will also be cancelled. Agree?"

Sid agreed.

"And you both will have to submit all your original mark sheets and documents to company HR office. We will not give it back up to the years mentioned in this legal bond. It could be for five years at least." said Sujoy Sir.

"Sure Sir. I agree."

29.

On that happy and sweet moment, I was waiting outside the yellow STD booth to call my Dad. Someone, an over-talkative man was already there inside the booth.

My thoughts travelled on remembering my last semester in which Sid had touched and changed all the dimensions of my life. Without touching me physically, he got involved with my sexuality by his erotic audio stories, he introduced me to love by the story of the tree and a child, and he took me beyond love by Draupadi-Krishna's friendship story.

I told myself,

"But, now what? What about my future with him!

Is Sid a kind of person who can do a nine to five job?

Does he believe in marriage?

Just because he weaved that story of tree and a child, should I think that he has the deep insight of love? No. I don't think so. He is a professional storyteller. He earns from it. He is more of brain and less of heart.

If I consider him as an experiment, then, in that context, I am just a theory.

Can we fit in?

Who changes who?

And how much?

I should worry about these important questions. But no. Now I am a changed person. Just now, Sid has shared a *paan* with me. My lips and mouth are reddish by that shared thing and not by any artificial color of lipstick. Smell of *qimam* is not allowing me to worry about anything. It is keeping me inside Sid's careless attitude."

I tried to think what would have happened if Sid had never entered my life. I couldn't find it any better. Yet there was a challenge in front of me. I had to score 88% in final semester.

"Shama, I have calculated your average from mark sheet. You need to score 88% in this semester's exam itself," said Sid. There was no worry on his face. He didn't surprise me. He always kept information about me.

"I think it's impossible to score," I said.

"Your selection in the interview was also impossible. But, it happened. Isn't it? And yes, it's impossible to score 88% if you want to depend on chits and Ravin. Otherwise I can help you. Yet, we have twenty four days before the final exam. Let's plan to score above 90%. I want to see we both, flying first flight to Pune, where we will be posted in Lupin Research Park."

With that offer, he planted a seed of dream inside me. I could imagine myself with him in a domestic flight from Vadodara to Pune. My eyes filled with a dream. A dream, which was unthinkable for me. Sid's words were bringing it in my hands within no time.

One thing I perfectly understood was that without Sid, I would never manage to have control over my own life. I would have married someone and would have become a secondary thing of him.

"Sid…Sid…" I couldn't utter any more words. I was looking at him. But, my vision became blurred because of tears which were there. They hadn't started flowing.

He came nearer. He waited for something from me.

"I want to fly with you. But…" I said.

"Hmmm… but what?" Sid said.

"Not in economy class. Please book our first flight in business class," I said. My dreams had started growing bigger.

He hugged me tightly. And after a while, he loosened his grip to let me breath. He took my face in between his palms. He completed that unfinished kiss which was started in that dark corner of library. My tears had found way to flow. My tears added a new taste during our prolonged kiss. We invested equally to create the kiss which Sid was used to call "vacuum kiss".

Unthinkable things were in my hands. I was about to share a happy moment with my dad. I was glowing with magical colors of dreams.

That over-talkative man inside the STD booth had left now.

"Don't miss me while I'm going inside," I said, walking towards booth.

"No point of missing. I'm coming with you inside," he said.

I said him no, widening my eyes. He gently pressed his handkerchief on my teary eyes. He planted a kiss before letting me go to phone.

I kept composing and deleting sentences inside my mind- the best frame of words, I should utter to announce my selection in Lupin on phone call. I was sure that my dad has waited for this moment far more than me.

I remembered his last words at the bus station. He had said, "One should always give chance whoever keeps providing "one more chance" back."

I have found a boy who had given me a chance to make a life in spite of my three consistently poor mark sheets and my sick ways to get settled.

I pressed numbers on that overused dial pad of STD phone. My dad attended a call before a first ring finished. I recognized his voice but couldn't understand his words. There was a network problem. I cut the call and dialed again. This time he took time to attend. I heard my mother's voice. It was clear voice now.

"Can you hear me?" said my mother.

"Yes Mamma. Where is dad?"

"Yes *Beta*! I am here. Tell me." She had given to him now.

"Lupin…campus interview…I have been selected under their special program young leaders program," I said. I hadn't any properly composed sentence.

"Finally…congratulations…which city?" he said. It felt as if he was speechless. He was talking in very low and tired voice.

"In Pune. Lupin Research Park. But, what happened to you? I mean your voice…"

"It's too difficult to postpone heart attack, *Beta*. I waited so long for this moment from you. Go ahead. Claim on your dreams. And… and thank you. You have given me freedom at the perfect time."

And then, I heard a voice …thakaak…thakaak… as if phone receiver would have fallen from his hand. Within no time, I heard crying voice of lot of women. No one cared to answer me anything from that fallen receiver.

“Hello… hello… Dad? Are you there? Please say something. Dad!”

Presence of dead body controlled everything around. My dad was quite right. He had said, “Death speaks louder than life.”

I started feeling nauseous.

Before I fell down, Sid came inside and held me.

Held my whole existence, in that small, suffocating, wooden yellow STD booth.